The Unexpe

Algis Budrys was born in East Prussia in 1931 and moved to the United States in 1936 when his father became Representative of the Lithuanian Government-in-Exile. He entered publishing in the early 1950s, becoming Assistant Editor with Galaxy Publications and later Editorial Director of Playboy Press. He sold his first short story in 1952 and his novels include *Who?* (1958), *Rogue Moon* (1960), *The Iron Thorn* (1967) and *Michaelmas* (1977).

The
Unexpected
Dimension

Algis Budrys

Fontana/Collins

To: Frederik Pohl

First published in the USA by Ballantine Books, 1960
First published in Great Britain by Victor Gollancz, 1962
First issued in Fontana 1979

THE END OF SUMMER, © copyright 1954 by Street & Smith Publications, Inc., first appeared in *Astounding Science Fiction*. Reprinted by permission of the author's agent.
THE DISTANT SOUND OF ENGINES, © copyright 1959 by Mercury Press Inc., first appeared in *The Magazine of Fantasy and Science Fiction*. Reprinted by permission of the author's agent.
NEVER MEET AGAIN, © copyright 1957 by Royal Publications, Inc., first appeared in *Infinity Science Fiction*. Reprinted by permission of the author's agent.
THE BURNING WORLD, © copyright 1957 by Royal Publications, Inc., first appeared in *Infinity Science Fiction*. Reprinted by permission of the author's agent.
FIRST TO SERVE, © copyright 1954 by Street & Smith Publications, Inc., first appeared in *Astounding Science Fiction*. Reprinted by permission of the author's agent.
GO AND BEHOLD THEM, © copyright 1958 by Fantasy House, Inc., first appeared in *Venture Science Fiction*. Reprinted by permission of the author's agent.
THE EXECUTIONER, © copyright 1955 by Street & Smith Publications, Inc., first appeared in *Astounding Science Fiction*. Reprinted by permission of the author's agent.

Made and printed in Great Britain by
Love and Malcomson Ltd., Brighton Road,
Redhill, Surrey

Contents

The End of Summer

I

Americaport hadn't changed since he'd last seen it, two hundred years before. It was set as far away from any other civilized area as possible, so that no plane, no matter how badly strayed, could possibly miss its landing and crash into a dwelling. Except for the straight-edge swath of the highway leading south, it was completely isolated if you forgot the almost deserted tube station. Its edge was dotted by hangars and a few offices, but the terminal building itself was small, and severely functional. Massive with bare concrete, aseptic with steel and aluminium, it was a gray, bleak place in the wilderness.

Kester Fay was so glad to see it that he jumped impatiently from the big jet's passenger lift. He knew he was getting curious looks from the ground crew clustered around the stainless-steel ship, but he would have been stared at in any case, and he had seen the sports car parked and waiting for him beside the Administration Building. He hurried across the field at a pace that attracted still more attention, eager to get his clearance and be off.

He swung his memory vault impatiently by the chain from his wristlet while the Landing Clearance officer checked his passport, but the man was obviously too glad to see someone outside the small circle of airlines personnel. He stalled interminably, and while Fay had no doubt that his life out here bored him to tears, it was becoming harder and harder to submit patiently.

'Christopher Jordan Fay,' the man read off, searching for a fresh conversational opening. 'Well, Mr Fay, we haven't seen you here since '753. Enjoy your stay?'

'Yes,' he answered as shortly as possible. Enjoyed it? Well, yes, he supposed he had, but it was hard to feel that way since he'd played his old American memories at augmented volume all through the flight across the Atlantic.

Lord, but he was tired of Europe at this moment; weary of winding grassy lanes that meandered with classic patience among brooks and along creeks, under old stately trees! 'It's good to be back where a man can stretch his legs, though.'

The official chuckled politely, stamping forms. 'I'll bet it is at that. Planning to stay long?'

Forever, if I can help it, Fay thought first. But then he smiled ruefully. His life had already been an overdone demonstration that forever was a long time. 'For a while, at any rate,' he answered, his impatience growing as he thought of the car again. He shuffled his feet on the case-hardened flooring.

'Shall I arrange for transportation to New York?'

Fay shook his head. 'Not for me. But the man who drove my car up might be a customer.'

The official's eyebrows rose, and Fay suddenly remembered that America, with its more liberal social attitudes, might tolerate him more than Europe had, but that there were still plenty of conservatives sheltered under the same banner.

As a matter of fact, he should have realized that the official was a Homebody; a Civil Service man, no doubt. Even with a dozen safe places to put it down within easy reach, he still kept his memory vault chained to his wrist. Fay's own eyebrows lifted, and amusement glittered in his eyes.

'Driving down?' The official looked at Fay with a mixtur of respect, envy, and disapproval.

'It's only fifteen hundred miles,' Fay said with careful nonchalance. Actually, he felt quite sure that he was going to throttle the man if he wasn't let out of here and behind the wheel soon. But it would never do to be anything but bored in front of a Homebody. 'I expect to make it in about three days,' he added, almost yawning.

'Yes, sir,' the man said, instantly wrapping himself in a mantle of aloof politeness, but muttering 'Dilly!' almost audibly.

Fay'd hit home with that one, all right! Probably, the man had never set foot in an automobile. Certainly, he considered it a barefaced lie that anyone would undertake to average fifty mph during a driving day. Safe, cushiony pneumocars were his speed – and he an airlines employee!

Fay caught himself hastily. Everybody had a right to live any way he wanted to, he reminded himself.

But he could not restrain an effervescent grin at the man's sudden injured shift to aloofness.

'All right, sir,' the official said crisply, returning Fay's passport. 'Here you are. No baggage, of course?'

'Of course,' Fay said agreeably, and if that had been intended as a slur at people who traveled light and fast, it had fallen exceedingly flat. He waved his hand cheerfully as he turned away, while the official stared at him sourly. 'I'll be seeing you again, I imagine.'

'I'm afraid not, sir,' the man answered with a trace of malevolence. 'United States Lines is shutting down passenger service the first of next dekayear.'

Momentarily nonplussed, Fay hesitated. 'Oh? Too bad. No point to continuing, though, is there?'

'No, sir. I believe you were our first in a hectoyear and a half.' Quite obviously, he considered that as much of a mark of Cain as necessary.

'Well . . . must be dull out here, eh?'

He cocked a satiric eye at the man and was gone, chuckling at that telling blow while the massive exit door swung ponderously shut behind him.

The car's driver was obviously a Worker who'd taken on the job because he needed money for some obscure, Workerish purpose. Fay settled the business in the shortest possible time, counting out hundred-dollar bills with a rapid shuffle. He threw in another for good measure, and waved the man aside, punching the starter vibrantly. He was back, he was home! He inhaled deeply, breathing the untrammeled air.

Curled around mountains and trailed gently through valleys, the road down through New York State was a joy.

Fay drove it with a light, appreciative smile, guiding his car exuberantly, his muscles locked into communion with the automobile's grace and power as his body responded to each banked turn, each surge of acceleration below the downward crest of a hill. There was nothing like this in Europe – nothing. Over there, they left no room for his kind among their stately people.

He had almost forgotten what it was like to sit low behind the windscreen of a two-seater and listen to the dancing explosions of the unmuffled engine. It was good to be back, here on this open, magnificent road, with nothing before or behind but satin-smooth ferroconcrete, and heaped green mountains to either side.

He was alone on the road, but thought nothing of it. There were very few who lived his kind of life. Now that his first impatience had passed, he was sorry he hadn't been able to talk to the jet's pilot. But that, of course, had been out of the question. Even with all the safety interlocks, there was the chance that one moment's attention lost would allow an accident to happen.

So, Fay had spent the trip playing his memory on the plane's excellent equipment, alone in the comfortable but small compartment forward of the ship's big cargo cabin.

He shrugged as he nudged the car around a curve in the valley. It couldn't be helped. It was a lonely life, and that was all there was to it. He wished there were more people who understood that it was the *only* life – the only solution to the problem which had fragmented them into so many social patterns. But there were not. And, he supposed, they were all equally lonely. The Homebodies, the Workers, the Students, and the Teachers. Even, he conceded, the Hoppers. He'd Hopped once himself, as an experiment. It had been a hollow, hysteric experience.

The road straightened, and, some distance ahead, he saw the white surface change to the dark macadam of an urban district. He slowed in response, considering the advisability of switching his safeties in, and decided it was unnecessary as yet. He disliked being no more than a pea in a safetied car's basket, powerless to do anything but sit with his hands and feet off the controls. No; for another moment, he wanted to be free to turn the car nearer the shoulder and drive through the shade of the thick shrubbery and overhanging trees. He breathed deeply of the faint fragrance in the air and once more told himself that *this* was the only way to live, the only way to find some measure of vitality. A Dilly? Only in the jealous vocabularies of the Homebodies, so long tied to their hutches and routines that the scope of mind and emotion had narrowed to fit their microcosm.

Then, without warning, still well on the white surface of open road, the brown shadow darted out of the bushes and flung itself at his wheels, barking shrilly.

He tried to snap the car out of the way, his face suddenly white, but the dog moved unpredictably, its abrupt yell of pain louder than the scream of Fay's brakes. He felt the soft bump, and then his foot jerked away from the clutch and the car stalled convulsively. Even with his engine dead and the car still, he heard no further sound from the dog.

Then he saw the Homebody boy running toward him up the road, and the expression of his face changed from shocked unpleasantness to remorseful regret. He sighed and climbed out of the car clumsily, trying to think of something to say.

The boy came running up and stopped beside the car, looking up the road with his face drawn into tearful anger.

'You *ran* over Brownie!'

Fay stared helplessly down at the boy. 'I'm sorry, son,' he said as gently as he could. He could think of nothing really meaningful to tell him. It was a hopeless situation. 'I . . . I shouldn't have been driving so fast.'

The boy ran to the huddled bundle at the shoulder of the road and picked it up in his arms, sobbing. Fay followed him, thinking that ten thousand years of experience were not enough – that a hundred centuries of learning and acquiring superficial maturity were still insufficient to shield the emotions trapped in a young boy's body, at the mercy of his glandular system, under a shock like this.

'Couldn't you see him?' the boy pleaded.

Fay shook his head numbly. 'He came out of the shrubs — '

'You shouldn't have been driving so fast. You should have — '

'I know.' He looked uselessly back up the road, the trees bright green in the sunshine, the sky blue.

'I'm sorry,' he told the boy again. He searched desperately for something, some way, to make recompense. 'I wish it hadn't happened.' He thought of something, finally. 'I . . . I know it wouldn't be the same thing, but I've got a dog of my own – a basset hound. He's coming over from Europe on a cargo ship. When he gets here, would you like to have him?'

'Your *own* dog?' For a moment, the boy's eyes cleared, but then he shook his head hopelessly. 'It wouldn't work out,' he said simply, and then, as though conscious of guilt at even considering that any other dog could replace his, tightened his arms on the lifeless bundle.

No, it hadn't been such a good idea, Fay realized. If he weren't so snarled up in remorse and confusion, he'd have seen that. Ugly had been his dog and couldn't be separated from him, or he from Ugly. He realized even more strongly just precisely what he had done to the boy.

'Something wrong? Oh — ' The Homebody man who had come up the road stopped beside them. his face turning grave. Fay looked at him in relief.

'I had my automatics off,' he explained to the man. 'I wouldn't have, if I'd known there was a house around here, but I didn't see anything. I'm terribly sorry about the . . . about Brownie.'

The man looked again at the dog in the boy's arms, and winced. Then he sighed and shrugged helplessly. 'Guess it was bound to happen sometime. Should have been on a leash. There's still a law of averages.'

Fay's fist clenched behind his back, out of sight. The well-worn words bit deep at the very foundation of his vitality, and his mind bridled, but in another moment the spasm of reflexive fear was gone, and he was glad he'd had this harmless outlet for his emotions. Besides, the man was right, and at this moment Fay was forced to be honest enough with himself to admit it. There was still a law of averages, whether Fay and his Dilly kind liked it or not.

'Go on back to the house, son,' the man said with another sigh. 'There's nothing we can do for Brownie. We'll bury him later. Right now you ought to wash up. I'll be along in a minute.'

It was the way he said it – the fatalistic acceptance that no matter what the honest folk did, some blundering, heedless dilettante was going to thwart them – that scored Fay's emotions.

The boy nodded wordlessly, still crying, and began to walk away without looking at Fay again.

But Fay couldn't let him go. Like a man who picks at a splinter, he could not let this pass so simply. 'Wait!' he said urgently.

The boy stopped and looked at him woodenly.

'I . . . I know there's nothing – I mean,' Fay stumbled, 'Brownie was your dog, and there can't be another one like him. But I do a lot of traveling — ' He stopped again, flushing at the Homebody man's knowing look, then pushed on regardless. 'I see a lot of people,' he went on. 'I'll try to find you a dog that hasn't ever belonged to anybody. When I do, I'll bring him to you. I promise.'

The boy's lip twitched, suddenly revealing what ten thousand years had taught him. 'Thanks, mister,' he said half-scornfully, and walked away, cradling his dog.

He hadn't believed him, of course. Fay suddenly realized that no one ever believed a Dilly, whether he was telling the truth or not. He realized, too, that he had done the best he could, and nevertheless failed. He looked regretfully after the boy.

'You didn't have to do that,' the man said softly, and Fay noted that some of his reserve and half-contemptuous politeness were gone. 'I don't know whether to believe you

13

or not, but you didn't have to do that. Anyway, I'll edit the dog out of his memories tonight. My wife and I'll clean the place up, and he won't notice anything.' He paused, reflecting, his eyes dark. 'Guess Madge and I'll cut it out of our own minitapes, too.'

Fay clenched his teeth in sudden annoyance. Nobody ever believed a Dilly. 'No,' he said. 'I wish you wouldn't do that. I meant what I said.' He shook his head again. 'I don't like editing. There's always a slip somewhere, and then you know you've got a hole in your memory, but you can never remember what it was.'

The man looked at him curiously. 'Funny thing for one of you people to say. I always heard you went for editing in a big way.'

Fay kept his face from showing his thoughts. There it was again – that basic lack of understanding and a complete unwillingness to check secondhand tales. The very essence of his kind of life was that no memory, no experience, not be lived and preserved. Besides, he'd always heard that it was the Homebodies who had to edit whole hectoyears to keep from going mad with boredom.

'No,' he contented himself with saying. 'You're confusing us with the Hoppers. *They'll* try anything.'

The man curled his lip at the mention, and Fay reflected that the introduction of a common outsider seemed helpful in circumstances like this.

'Well . . . maybe you're right,' the man said, still not completely trustful, but willing to take the chance. He gave Fay his name, Arnold Riker, and his address. Fay put the slip of paper carefully in his memory vault.

'Anytime I lose that, I'll have lost my memory, too,' he commented.

The man grinned wryly. 'More likely, you'll remember to forget it tonight,' he said, some of his distrust returning at the sight of the spooled tapes.

Fay took that without protest. He supposed Riker had a right to feel that way. 'Can I drive you down to your house?'

The man flicked an expressive glance along the car's length and shook his head. 'Thanks. I'll walk. There's still a law of averages.'

And you can take that phrase and carve it on Humanity's headstone, Fay thought bitterly, but did not reply.

He climbed into the car, flicked on the automatics, and froze, completely immobile from sharply ingrained habit that was the only way to avoid the careless move that just might open the safety switch. He did not even turn his head to look at the man he left behind as the car started itself slowly away, nor did he catch more than a passing glimpse of the house where the boy and his dog had lived together for ten kiloyears.

We guard our immortality so carefully, he thought. So very, very carefully. But there's still a law of averages.

II

Perversely, he drove more rapidly than normal for the rest of the trip. Perhaps he was trying to reaffirm his vitality. Perhaps he was running away. Perhaps he was trying to cut down the elapsed time between towns, where his automatics threaded him through the light pedestrian traffic and sent him farther down the road, with each new danger spot safely behind him. At any rate, he arrived at his Manhattan apartment while it was still daylight, stepping off the continuous-impulse elevator with some satisfaction. But his eyes were discontented.

The apartment, of course, was just as he had left it two hectoyears ago. The semirobots had kept it sealed and germicidal until the arrival of his return message yesterday.

He could imagine the activity that had followed, as books and music tapes were broken out of their helium-flooded vaults, rugs and furnishings were stripped of their cocoons, aerated, and put in place. From somewhere, new plants had come and been set in the old containers, and fresh liquor put in the cabinet. There would be food in the kitchen, clothes in the wardrobes – the latest styles, of

15

course, purchased with credits against the left-behind apparel of two hectoyears before – and there were the same, old, familiar paintings on the walls. Really old, not just By-Product stuff.

He smiled warmly as he looked around him, enjoying the swell of emotion at the apartment's comfortable familiarity. He smiled once more, briefly, at the thought that he must some day devise a means of staying in a sealed apartment – wearing something like a fishing lung, perhaps – and watch the semirobots at their refurbishing process. It must be a fascinating spectacle.

But his glance had fallen on the memory vault which he had unchained and put on a coffee table. It faced him with the ageless, silent injunction painted on each of its faces: PLAY ME, and underneath this the block of smaller lettering that he, like everyone else, knew by heart:

If your surroundings seem unfamiliar, or you have any other reason to suspect that your environment and situation are not usual, request immediate assistance from any other individual. He is obligated by strict law to direct you to the nearest free public playback booth, where you will find further instructions. Do not be alarmed, and follow these directions without anxiety, even if they seem strange to you. In extreme situations, stand still and do not move. Hold this box in front of you with both hands. This is a universally recognized signal of distress. Do not let anyone take this box away from you, no matter what the excuse offered.

He wondered momentarily what had made him notice it; he knew it so well that the pattern of type had long ago become no more than a half-seen design with a recognition value so high that it had lost all verbal significance.

Was it some sort of subconscious warning? He checked his memory hastily, but relaxed when he found none of the tell-tale vagueness of detail that meant it was time to let everything else wait and get to a playback as fast as possible. He had refreshed his memory early this morning, before starting the last leg of his trip, and it seemed to be good for several more hours, at least.

What was it, then?

He frowned and went to the liquor cabinet, wondering if some train of thought had been triggered off by the accident and was trying to call attention to himself. And when he dropped into an easy-chair a few minutes later, a drink in his hand and his eyes still brooding over the vault's legend, he realized that his second guess had been the right one. As usual, one level of his mind had been busy digesting while the surface churned in seeming confusion.

He smiled ruefully. Maybe he wasn't quite as much of a Dilly as he looked and would have liked to believe. Still, a man couldn't live ten thousand years and not put a few things together in his head. He took a sip of his drink and stared out over the city in the gathering twilight. Somewhere in the graceful furniture behind him, a photoelectric relay clicked, and his high-fidelity set began to play the Karinius *Missa*. The apartment had not forgotten his moods.

No, he thought, the machines never forgot. Only men forgot, and depended on machines to help them remember. He stared at the vault, and a familiar sophistry occurred to him. 'Well,' he asked the box labeled PLAY ME, 'which *is* my brain – you or the gray lump in my head?'

The answer depended on his moods, and on his various audiences. Tonight, alone, in an uncertain mood, he had no answer.

He took another drink and sat back, frowning.

At best, he'd offered the boy a shoddy substitute. Even presuming that the passage of ten kiloyears had somehow still left room for a dog without a master, the animal would have to be re-familiarized with the boy at least once or twice a day.

Why? Why did dogs who had always had the same master remember him without any difficulty, even though they seemed to have to reinvestigate their surroundings periodically? Why would Ugly, for instance, remember him

17

joyfully when his ship came? And why would Ugly have to be re-familiarized with this apartment, in which he'd lived with Fay, off and on, for all this time?

The Kinnard dog, whose master insisted on building each new house in a carbon-copy of the previous, didn't have anywhere near as much trouble. Why?

He'd heard rumors that some people were recording canine memories on minitape, but that sort of story was generally classified along with the jokes about the old virgin who switched vaults with her nubile young niece.

Still and all, there might be something in that. He'd have to ask Monkreeve. Monkreeve was the Grand Old Man of the crowd. He had memories the rest of them hadn't even thought of yet.

Fay emptied his glass and got up to mix another drink. He was thinking harder than he had for a long time – and he could not help feeling that he was making a fool of himself. Nobody else had ever asked questions like this. Not where others could hear them, at any rate.

He sat back down in his chair, fingers laced around the glass while the *Missa* ended and the *Lieutenant Kije* suite caught up the tempo of the city as it quickened beneath showers of neon.

PLAY ME. Like a music tape, the memory vault held his life tightly knit in the nested spindles of bright, imperishable minitape.

What, he suddenly asked himself, would happen if he didn't play it tonight?

'If your surroundings seem unfamiliar, or you have any other reason to suspect your environment and situation are not usual . . .

'Obligated by strict law to direct you . . .

'Do not be alarmed . . .'

What? What was behind the whispered stories, the jokes:

'What did the girl in the playback booth say to the young man who walked in by mistake?

'Man, this has been the *busiest* Twenty-seventh of July!' (Laughter)

18

The thought struck him that there might be all sorts of information concealed in his fund of party conversation.

'If you wish to get to heaven,
Stay away from twenty-seven.'

And there it was again. Twenty-seven. July Twenty-seventh, this time conglomerated with a hangover reference to religion. And that was interesting, too. Man had religions, of course – schismatic trace sects that offered no universally appealing reward to make them really popular. But they must have been really big once, judging by the stamp they'd left on oaths and idiomatic expressions. Why? What did they have? Why had two billion people integrated words like 'Heaven,' 'Lord God,' and 'Christ' into the language so thoroughly that they had endured ten kiloyears?

July Twenty-seventh when? Year?

What would happen to him if he ignored PLAY ME just this once?

He had the feeling that he knew all this; that he had learned it at the same time that he had learned to comb his hair and cut his fingernails, take showers and brush his teeth. But he did all that more or less automatically now.

Maybe it was time he thought about it.

But nobody else did. Not even Monkreeve.

So what? Who was Monkreeve, really? Didn't the very fact that he had thought of it make it all right? That *was* the basis on which they judged everything else, wasn't it?

That boy and his dog had really started something.

He realized several things simultaneously, and set his glass down with a quick *thump*. He couldn't remember the dog's name. And he was definitely letting the simple problem of following his conscience – and his wounded pride – lead him into far deeper intellectual waters than any boy and his dog had a right.

His cheeks went cold as he tried to remember the name of this morning's hotel, and he shivered violently. He looked at the box labeled PLAY ME.

'Yes,' he told it. 'Yes, definitely.'

Fay awoke to a bright, sunny morning. The date on his calendar clock was April 16, 11958, and he grinned at it while he removed the vault's contacts from the bare places on his scalp. He noted that all the memories he had brought back from Europe had been re-recorded for the apartment's spare vault, and that the current minitape had advanced the shining notch necessary to record yesterday.

He looked at that notch and frowned. It looked like an editing scratch, and was. It was always there, every morning, but he knew it covered nothing more than the normal Traumatic pause between recording and playback. He'd been told that it was the one memory nobody wanted to keep, and certainly he'd never missed editing it – or, of course, remembered doing it. It was a normal part of the hypnotic action pattern set by the recorder to guide him when he switched over from record to playback, his mind practically blank by that time.

He'd never seen a tape, no matter whose, that did not bear that one scratch to mark each day. He took pride in the fact that a good many tapes were so hashed out and romanticized as to be almost pure fiction. He hadn't been lying to the boy's father – and he noted the presence of that memory with the utmost satisfaction – he had a driving basic need to see everything, hear everything, sense each day and its events to their fullest, and to remember them with sharp perfect clarity.

He laughed at the vault as he kicked it shut on his way to the bathroom. 'Not until tonight,' he said to PLAY ME, and then teetered for a breathless moment as he struggled to regain his balance. He set his foot down with a laugh, his eyes sparkling.

'Who needs a car to live dangerously?' he asked himself. But that brought back the memory of the boy, and his lips straightened. Nevertheless, it was a beautiful day, and the basic depression of yesterday was gone. He thought of all the people he knew in the city, one of whom, at least, would be sure to have a contact somewhere or the other that would solve his problem for him.

He ate his breakfast heartily, soaking for an hour in the sensual grip of his bathtub's safety slinging while he spooned the vitalizing porridge, then shrugged into a violent bathrobe and began calling people on the telephone.

He hadn't realized how long he'd been gone, he reflected, after Vera, his welcome to her apartment finished, had left him with a drink while she changed. It was, of course, only natural that some of the old crowd had changed their habits or themselves gone traveling in his absence. Nevertheless, he still felt a little taken aback at the old phone numbers that were no longer valid, or the really astonishing amount of people who seemed to have edited him out of their memories. Kinnard, of all people! And Lorraine.

Somehow he'd never thought Lorraine would go editor.

'Ready, Kes?'

Vera was wearing a really amazing dress. Apparently, America had gone back toward conservatism, as he might have guessed from his own wardrobe.

Vera, too, had changed somehow – too subtly for him to detect, here in surroundings where he had never seen her before. Hadn't she always been resistant to the fad of completely doing apartments over every seventy years? He seemed to remember it that way, but even with minitapes, the evidence of the eye always took precedence over the nudge of memory. Still, she at least knew where Monkreeve was, which was something he hadn't been able to find out for himself.

'Uh-huh. Where're we going?'

She smiled and kissed the tip of his nose. 'Relax, Kes. Let it happen.'

Um.

'Grasshoppers as distinct from ants, people given to dancing and similar gay pursuits, or devotees to stimulants,' Monkreeve babbled, gesturing extravagantly. 'Take your pick of derivations.' He washed down a pill of some sort

21

and braced himself theatrically. 'I've given up on the etymology. What'd you say your name was?'

Fay grimaced. He disliked Hoppers and Hopper parties – particularly in this instance. He wished heartily that Vera had told him what had happened to Monkreeve before she brought him here.

He caught a glimpse of her in the center of an hysterical knot of people, dancing with her seven petticoats held high.

'Woee!' Monkreeve burst out, detecting the effects of the pill among the other explosions in his system. Fay gave him a searching look, and decided, from the size of his pupils, that he could probably convince himself into an identical state on bread pills, and more than likely was.

'Got a problem, hey, Lad?' Monkreeve asked wildly. 'Got a dog problem.' He put his finger in his mouth and burlesqued Thought. 'Got a dog, got a problem, got a problem, got a dog,' he chanted. 'Hell!' he exploded, 'go see old Williamson. Old Williamson knows everything. Ask him anything. Say,' he snickered, 'ask him anything.'

'Thanks, Monk,' Fay said. 'Glad to've met you,' he added in the accepted polite form with editors, and moved toward Vera.

'Sure, sure, Kid. Ditto and check. Whatcha say your name was?'

Fay pretended to be out of earshot, brushed by a couple who were dancing in a tight circle to no music at all, and delved into the crowd around Vera.

'Hi, Kes!' Vera exclaimed, looking up and laughing. 'Did Monk give you any leads?'

'Monk has a monkey on his back, he thinks,' Fay said shortly, a queasy feeling in his throat.

'Well, why not try that on the kid? He might like a change.' Vera broke into fresh laughter. Suddenly an inspiration came to her, and she began to sing.

'Oh where, oh where, has my little dog gone? Oh where, oh where can he be?'

The rest of the crowd picked it up. Vera must have told them about his search, for they sang it with uproarious gusto.

Fay turned on his heel and walked out.

The halls of the University library were dim gray, padded with plastic sponge, curving gently with no sharp corners. Doorways slid into walls, the sponge muffled sound, and he wore issued clothes into which he had been allowed to transfer only those personal items which could not possibly cut or pry. Even his vault had been encased in a ball of cellular sponge plastic, and his guide stayed carefully away from him, in case he should fall or stumble. The guide carried a first-aid kit, and like all the library staff, was a certified Doctor of Theoretical Medicine.

'This is Dr Williamson's interview chamber,' the guide told him softly, and pressed a button concealed under the sponge. The door slid back, and Fay stepped into the padded interior of the chamber, divided down the middle by a sheet of clear, thick plastic. There was no furniture to bump into, of course. The guide made sure he was safely in, out of the door's track, and closed it carefully after he had stepped out.

Fay sat down on the soft floor and waited. He started wondering what had happened to the old crowd, but he had barely found time to begin when the door on the other side of the partition opened and Dr Williamson came in. Oddly enough, his physiological age was less than Fay's, but he carried himself like an old man, and his entire manner radiated the same feeling.

He looked at Fay distastefully. 'Hopper, isn't it? What're you doing here?'

Fay got to his feet. 'No, sir. Dilly, if you will, but not a Hopper.' Coming so soon after the party, Williamson's remark bit deep.

'Six of one, half a dozen of the other, in time,' Williamson said curtly. 'Sit down.' He lowered himself slowly, testing each new adjustment of his muscles and bones before he made the next. He winced faintly when Fay dropped to the floor with defiant overcarelessness. 'Well – go on. You wouldn't be here if the front desk didn't think your research was at least interesting.'

Fay surveyed him carefully before he answered. Then he sighed, shrugged mentally, and began. 'I want to find a dog for a little boy,' he said, feeling more than foolish.

Williamson snorted: 'What leads you to believe this is the ASPCA?'

'ASPCA, sir?'

Williamson threw his hands carefully up to heaven and snorted again. Apparently, everything Fay said served to confirm some judgment of mankind on his part.

He did not explain, and Fay finally decided he was waiting. There was a minute's pause, and then Fay said awkwardly: 'I assume that's some kind of animal shelter. But that wouldn't serve my purpose. I need a dog that . . . that *remembers*.'

Williamson put the tips of his fingers together and pursed his lips. 'So. A dog that remembers, eh?' He looked at Fay with considerably more interest, the look in his eyes sharpening.

'You look like any other brainless jackanapes,' he mused, 'but apparently there's some gray matter left in your artfully coiffed skull after all.' Williamson was partially bald.

'What would you say,' Williamson continued, 'if I offered to let you enroll here as an Apprentice Liberor?'

'Would I find out how to get that kind of dog?'

A flicker of impatience crossed Williamson's face. 'In time, in time. But that's beside the point.'

'I . . . I haven't got much time, sir,' Fay said haltingly. Obviously, Williamson had the answer to his question. But would he part with it, and if he was going to, why this rigmarole?

Williamson gestured with careful impatience. 'Time is unimportant. And especially here, where we avoid the law of averages almost entirely. But there are various uses for time, and I have better ones than this. Will you enroll? Quick, man!'

'I – Dr Williamson, I'm grateful for your offer, but right now all I'd like to know is how to get a dog.' Fay was conscious of a mounting impatience of his own.

Williamson got carefully to his feet and looked at Fay with barely suppressed anger.

'Young man, you're living proof that our basic policy is right. I wouldn't trust an ignoramus like you with the information required to cut his throat.

'Do you realize where you are?' He gestured at the walls. 'In this building is the world's greatest repository of knowledge. For ten thousand years we have been accumulating opinion and further theoretical data on every known scientific and artistic theory extant in 1973. We have data that will enable Man to go to the stars, travel ocean bottoms, and explore Jupiter. We have here the raw material of symphonies and sonatas that make your current addictions sound like a tincup beggar's fiddle. We have the seed of paintings that would make you spatter whitewash over the daubs you treasure, and verse that would drive you mad. And you want me to find you a dog!'

Fay had gotten to his own feet. Williamson's anger washed over him in battering waves, but one thing remained clear, and he kept to it stubbornly.

'Then you won't tell me.'

'No, I will *not* tell you! I thought for a moment that you had actually managed to perceive something of your environment, but you have demonstrated my error. You are dismissed.' Williamson turned and stamped carefully out of his half of the interview chamber, and the door slid open behind Fay.

Still and all, he had learned something. He had learned that there was something important about dogs not remembering, and he had a date: 1973.

He sat in his apartment, his eyes once more fixed on PLAY ME, and tried a thought on for size: July 27, 1973.

It made more sense that way than it did when the two parts were separated – which could mean nothing, of course. Dates were like the jigsaw puzzles that were manufactured for physiological four-year-olds: they fit together no matter how the pieces were matched.

When had the human race stopped having children?

The thought smashed him bolt upright in his chair, spilling his drink.

He had never thought of that. Never once had he questioned the fact that everyone was frozen at some apparently arbitrary physiological age. He had learned that such-and-such combined anatomical and psychological configuration was indicative of one physiological age, that a different configuration indicated another. Or had he? Couldn't he tell instinctively – or, rather, couldn't he tell as though the word 'age' were applicable to humans as well as inanimate objects?

A lesser thought followed close on the heels of the first: exactly the same thing could be said of dogs, or canaries or parakeets, as well as the occasional cat that hadn't gone wild.

'Gone' wild? Hadn't most cats always been wild?

Just exactly what memories were buried in his mind, in hiding – or rather, since he was basically honest with himself, what memories had he taught himself to ignore? And why?

His skin crawled. Suddenly, his careful, flower-to-flower world was tinged with frost around him, and brown, bare and sharply ragged stumps were left standing. The boy and his dog had been deep water indeed – for his tentative toe had baited a monster of continuous and expanding questions to fang him with rows of dangerous answers.

He shook himself and took another drink. He looked at PLAY ME, and knew where the worst answers must be.

IV

He awoke, and there were things stuck to his temples. He pulled them loose and sat up, staring at the furnishings and the machine that sat beside his bed, trailing wires.

The lights were on, but the illumination was so thoroughly diffused that he could not find its source. The furniture was just short of the radical in design, and he had certainly never worn pajamas to bed. He looked down at them and grunted.

He looked at the machine again, and he felt his temples where the contacts had rested. His fingers came away sticky, and he frowned. Was it some sort of encephalograph? Why?

He looked around again. There was a faint possibility that he was recovering from psychiatric treatment, but this was certainly no sanatorium room.

There was a white placard across the room, with some sort of printing on it. Since it offered the only possible course of information, he got off the bed cautiously and, when he encountered no dizziness or weakness, crossed over to it. He stood looking at it, lips pursed and brow furrowed, while he picked his way through the rather simplified orthography.

Christopher Jordan Fay:

If your surroundings seem unfamiliar, or you have any other reason to suspect that your environment and situation are unusual, do not be alarmed, and follow these directions without anxiety, even if they seem strange to you. If you find yourself unable to do so, for any reason whatsoever, please return to the bed and read the instructions printed on the machine beside it. In this case, the nearest 'free public playback booth' is the supplementary cabinet you see built into the head of the bed. Open the doors and read the supplementary instructions printed inside. In any case, do not be alarmed, and if you are unable or unwilling to perform any of the actions requested above, simply dial 'O' on the telephone you see across the room.

Fay looked around once more, identified the various objects, and read on.

The operator, like all citizens, is required by strict law to furnish you with assistance.

If, on the other hand, you feel sufficiently calm or are

commensurately curious, please follow these directions:

Return to the bed and restore the contacts to the places where they were attached. Switch the dial marked 'Record-Playback-Auxiliary Record' to the 'Auxiliary Record' position. You will then have three minutes to place your right forearm on the grooved portion atop the machine. Make certain your arm fits snugly – the groove is custom-molded to accept your arm perfectly in one position only.

Finally, lie back and relax. All other actions are automatic.

For your information, you have suffered from loss of memory, and this device will restore it to you.

Should you be willing to follow the above directions, please accept our thanks.

Fay's tongue bulged his left cheek, and he restrained a grin. Apparently, his generator had been an unqualified success. He looked at the printing again, just to be certain, and confirmed the suspicion that it had been done by his own hand. Then, as a conclusive check, he prowled the apartment in search of a calendar. He finally located the calendar-clock, inexpertly concealed in a bureau drawer, and looked at the date.

That was his only true surprise. He whistled shrilly at the date, but finally shrugged and put the clock back. He sat down in a convenient chair, and pondered.

The generator was working just as he'd expected, the signal bouncing off the heaviside layer without perceptible loss of strength, covering the Earth. As to what could happen when it exhausted its radio-active fuel in another five thousand years, he had no idea, but he suspected that he would simply refuel it. Apparently, he still had plenty of money, or whatever medium of exchange existed now. Well, he'd provided for it.

Interesting, how his mind kept insisting it was July 27 1973. This tendency to think of the actual date as 'the future' could be confusing if he didn't allow for it.

Actually, he was some ten-thousand-and-thirty-eight

28

years old, rather than the thirty-seven his mind insisted on. But his memories carried him only to 1973, while, he strongly suspected, the Kester who had written that naïve message had memories that *began* shortly thereafter.

The generator broadcast a signal which enabled body cells to repair themselves with one hundred per cent perfection, rather than the usual less-than-perfect of living organisms. The result was that none of the higher organisms aged, in any respect. Just the higher ones, fortunately, or there wouldn't even be yeast derivatives to eat.

But, of course, that included brain cells, too. Memory was a process of damaging brain cells much as a phonograph recording head damaged a blank record disk. In order to relive the memory, the organism had only to play it back, as a record is played. Except that, so long as the generator continued to put out the signal, brain cells, too, repaired themselves completely. Not immediately, of course, for the body took a little time to act. But no one could possibly sleep through a night and remember anything about the day before. Amnesia was the price of immortality.

He stood up, went to the liquor cabinet he'd located in his search, and mixed himself a drink, noticing again how little, actually, the world had progressed in ten thousand years. Cultural paralysis, more than likely, under the impact of two and a half billion individuals each trying to make his compromise with the essential boredom of eternal life. The drink was very good, the whiskey better than any he was used to. He envied himself.

They'd finally beaten amnesia, as he suspected the human race would. Probably by writing notes to themselves at first, while panic and hysteria cloaked the world and July 27th marched down through the seasons and astronomers went mad.

The stimulated cells, of course, did not repair the damage done to them before the generator went into operation. They took what they already had as a model, and clung to it fiercely.

He grimaced. Their improved encephalograph probably rammed in so much information so fast that their artificial memories blanketed the comparatively small amount of information which they had acquired up to the 27th. Or, somewhat more likely, the period of panic had been so bad that they refused to probe beyond it. If that was a tape-recording encephalograph, editing should be easily possible.

'I suspect,' he said aloud, 'that what I am remembering now is part of a large suppressed area in my own memory.' He chuckled at the thought that his entire life had been a blank to himself, and finished the drink.

And what he was experiencing now was an attempt on his own part to get that blank period on tape, circumventing the censors that kept him from doing it when he had his entire memory.

And that took courage. He mixed another drink and toasted himself. 'Here's to you, Kester Fay +. I'm glad to learn I've got guts.'

The whiskey was extremely good.

And the fact that Kester Fay had survived the traumatic hiatus between the Twenty-seventh and the time when he had his artificial memory was proof that They hadn't gotten to him before the smash-up.

Paranoid, was he?

He'd stopped the accelerating race toward Tee-Total War, hadn't he?

They hadn't been able to stop him, that was certain. He'd preserved the race of Man, hadn't he?

Psychotic? He finished the drink and chuckled. Intellectually, he had to admit that anyone who imposed immortality on all his fellow beings without asking their permission was begging for the label.

But, of course, he knew he wasn't psychotic. If he were, he wouldn't be so insistent on the English 'Kester' for a nickname rather than the American 'Chris'.

He put the glass down regretfully. Ah, well – time to give himself *all* his memories back. Why was his right arm so strong?

He lay down on the bed, replaced the contacts, and felt

30

the needle slip out of its recess in the forearm trough and slide into a vein.

Scopolamine derivative of some sort, he decided. Machinery hummed and clicked in the cabinets at the head of the bed, and a blank tape spindle popped into position in the vault, which rested on a specially-built stand beside the bed.

Complicated. he thought dimly as he felt the drug pumping into his system. I could probably streamline it down considerably.

He found time to think once more of his basic courage. Kester Fay must still be a rampant individual, even in his stagnant, conservative, ten-thousand-year-weighty civilization.

Apparently, nothing could change his fundamental character.

He sank into a coma with a faint smile.

The vault's volume control in the playback cycle was set to 'Emergency Overload'. Memories hammered at him ruthlessly, ravaging brain tissue, carving new channels through the packed silt of repair, foaming, bubbling, hissing with voracious energy and shattering impetus.

His face ran through agonized changes in his sleep. He pawed uncertainly and feebly at the contacts on his scalp, but the vital conditioning held. He never reached them, though he tried, and, failing, tried, and tried through the long night, while sweat poured down his face and soaked into his pillow, and he moaned, while the minitapes clicked and spun, one after the other, and gave him back the past.

It was July 27, 1973, and he shivered with cold, uncomprehendingly staring at the frost on the windows, with the note dated 7/27/73 in his hand.

It was July 27, 1973, and he was faint with hunger as he tried to get the lights to work. Apparently, the power was off. He struck a match and stared down at the series of notes, some of them smudged with much unremembered handling, all dated July 27, 1973.

It was July 27, 1973, and the men who tried to tell him

it was really Fall in 1989, clustered around his bed in the crowded hospital ward, were lying. But they told him his basic patents on controlled artificial radioactivity had made it possible to power the complicated machinery they were teaching him to use. And though, for some reason, money as an interest-gathering medium was no longer valid, they told him that in his special case, in gratitude, they'd arranged things so there'd be a series of royalties and licensing fees, which would be paid into his accounts automatically. He wouldn't even have to check on them, or know specifically where they came from. But the important part came when they assured him that the machinery – the 'vault', and the 'minitapes', whatever they were, would cure his trouble.

He was grateful for that, because he'd been afraid for a long time that he was going insane. Now he could forget his troubles.

Kester Fay pulled the vault contacts off his forehead and sat up to see if there was an editing scratch on the tape.

But, of course, there wasn't. He knew it before he'd raised his head an inch, and he almost collapsed, sitting on the edge of the bed with his head in his hands.

He was his own monster. He had no idea of what most of the words he'd used in those memories had meant, but even as he sat there, he could feel his mind hesitatingly making the linkages and assigning tags to the jumbled concepts and frightening rationalizations he'd already remembered.

He got up gingerly, and wandered about the apartment, straightening out the drawers he'd upset during his amnesiac period. He came to the empty glass, frowned at it, shrugged, and mixed a drink.

He felt better afterwards, the glow of 100 Proof working itself into his system. The effects wouldn't last, of course – intoxication was a result of damage to the brain cells – but the first kick was real enough. Moreover, it was all he'd gotten accustomed to, during the past ten kiloyears, just as the Hoppers could drug themselves eternally.

Ten thousand years of having a new personality seemed to have cured the psychosis he'd had with his old one. He felt absolutely no desire to change the world singlehanded.

Had it, now? Had it? Wasn't being a dilettante the result of an inner conviction that you were too good for routine living?

And didn't he want to turn the generator off, now that he knew what it did and where it was?

He finished the drink and bounced the glass in his palm. There was nothing that said he had to reach a decision right this minute. He'd had ten kiloyears. It could wait a little longer.

He bathed to the accompaniment of thoughts he'd always ignored before – thoughts about things that weren't his problem, then. Like incubators full of babies ten kiloyears old, and pregnant women, and paralytics.

He balanced that against hydrogen bombs, and still the scales did not tip.

Then he added something he had never known before, but that he had now, and understood why no one ever ventured to cross Twenty-seven, or to remember it if he had. For one instant, he, too, stopped still at his bath and considered ripping the memory out of his minitapes.

He added Death.

But he knew he was lost, now. For better or worse, the water had closed over his head, and if he edited the memory now, he would seek it out again some day. For a moment, he wondered if that was precisely what he had done, countless times before.

He gave it up. It could wait – if he stayed sane. At any rate, he knew how to get the little boy his dog, now.

He built a signal generator to cancel out the effect of the big one, purring implacably in its mountain shaft, sending out its eternal, unshieldable signal. He blanketed one room of his apartment with the canceling wave, and added six months to his age by staying in it for hours during the eighteen months it took to mate Ugly and raise the best

33

B

pup, for the stimulating wave was the answer to sterility, too. Fetuses could not develop.

He cut himself from the Dilly crowd, what was left of it, and raised the pup. And it was more than six months he added to his age, for all that time he debated and weighed, and remembered.

And by the time he was ready, he still did not know what he was going to do about the greater problem. Still and all, he had a new dog for the boy.

He packed the canceling generator and the dog in his car, and drove back up the road he had come.

Finally, he knocked on Riker's door, the dog under one arm, the generator under the other.

Riker answered his knock and looked at him curiously.

'I'm . . . I'm Kester Fay, Mr Riker,' he said hesitating. 'I've brought your boy that dog I promised.'

Riker looked at the dog and the bulky generator under his arm, and Fay shifted his load awkwardly, the dangling vault interfering with his movements. Light as it was, the vault was a bulky thing. 'Don't you remember me?'

Riker blinked thoughtfully, his forehead knotting. Then he shook his head. 'No . . . no, I guess not, Mr Fay.' He looked suspiciously at Fay's clothes, which hadn't been changed in three days. Then he nodded.

'Uh . . . I'm sorry, mister, but I guess I must have edited it.' He smiled in embarrassment. 'Come to think of it, I've wondered if we didn't have a dog sometime. I hope it wasn't too important to you.'

Fay looked at him. He found it impossible to think of anything to say. Finally, he shrugged.

'Well,' he said, 'your boy doesn't have a dog now, does he?'

Riker shook his head. 'Nope. You know – it's a funny thing, what with the editing and everything, but he knows a kid with a dog, and sometimes he pesters the life out of me to get him one.' Riker shrugged. 'You know how kids are.'

'Will you take this one?' He held out the squirming animal.

'Sure. Mighty grateful. But I guess we both know this won't work out too well.' He reached out and took the dog.

'This one sure will,' Fay said. He gave Riker the generator. 'Just turn this on for a while in the same room with your son and the dog. It won't hurt anything, but the dog'll remember.'

Riker looked at him skeptically.

'Try it,' Fay said, but Riker's eyes were narrowing, and he gave Fay both the dog and the generator back.

'No, thanks,' he said. 'I'm not trying anything like that from a guy that comes out of nowhere in the middle of the night.'

'Please, Mr Riker. I promise——'

'Buddy, you're trespassing. I won't draw more than half a hectoyear if I slug you.'

Fay's shoulders slumped. 'All right,' he sighed, and turned around. He heard Riker slam the heavy door behind him.

But as he trudged down the walk, his shoulders lifted, and his lips set in a line.

There has to be an end somewhere, he thought. Each thing has to end, or there will never be any room for beginnings. He turned around to be sure no one in the house was watching, and released the dog. He'd be found in the morning, and things might be different by then.

He climbed into the car and drove quickly away, leaving the dog behind. Somewhere outside of town, he threw the canceling generator outside, onto the concrete highway, and heard it smash. He unchained his memory vault, and threw it out, too.

There had to be an end. Even an end to starlit nights and the sound of a powerful motor. An end to the memory of sunset in the Piazza San Marco, and the sight of snow on Chamonix. An end to good whiskey. For him, there had to be an end – so that others could come after. He pointed the car towards the generator's location, and reflected that he had twenty or thirty years left, anyway.

He flexed his curiously light arm.

The Distant Sound of Engines

'Len? Lenny?' The unearthly man in the next bed was trying to wake me up.

I lay in the dark, my hands behind my head, listening to the traffic going by the hospital. Even late at night – and it was late whenever the man in the next bed dared to talk to me – the traffic outside was fairly heavy because the highway ran straight through town. That had been a lucky thing for me, because the ambulance attendant never had been able to stop the flow of blood out of my legs. Another half mile, another two minutes, and I would have been as dry as a cast-off snakeskin.

But I was all right, now, except that the jacknifing truck had taken my legs off under the dashboard. I was alive, and I could hear the trucks going by all night. The long, long rigs; semi-trailers, tandems, reefers . . . coming up the seaboard from Charleston and Norfolk, going on to New York . . . coming down from Boston, from Providence . . . Men I knew, driving them. Jack Biggs. Sam Lasovic. Tiny Morrs, with the ring finger of his right hand missing at the first joint. I was one up on Tiny, for sure.

Job in the dispatcher's office waiting for you, Lenny, I said to myself. No sweat. No more bad coffee, cold nights, sandpaper eyes. Getting a little old for the road, anyhow. Thirty-eight. Sure.

'Lenny . . .'

The best the man in the next bed would do was whisper. I wondered if he wasn't just afraid. He was afraid to talk at all in the daytime, because the nurses simply stuck a new needle in him every time he made a sound. Stuck it through a thin place in the bandages, they did, and walked away in a hurry. Sometimes they missed, and sometimes only some of the morphine got under his skin, so that only his arm went numb. The man in the next bed bragged about the times that happened. He tried to make them miss, moving his arms a little. Sometimes they noticed, but more often they didn't.

He didn't want the needle, the man in the next bed didn't. The needle took away the pain, and without the pain, with bandaging all over his face, he didn't have any proof he was alive. He was a stubborn, smart man, fighting back that way, because he'd developed a craving for the stuff, even not being like you and me. I mean, from some different place.

'*Lenny . . .*'

'Hunh?' I said, fogging my voice. I always made him wait. I didn't want him to know I stayed awake all night.

'Awake?'

'Now.'

'I'm sorry, Len.'

'Okay,' I said quickly. I didn't want him feeling obligated to me. 'It's all right. I get plenty of sleep daytimes.'

'Len. The formula for exceeding the velocity of light is . . .' And he began giving me the figures and letters.

Last night it had been the exact proportions of the metals in a high-temperature resistant alloy; the melting and pouring techniques for it; the hardening process. The night before, hull specifications. I listened until he was through.

'Have you got that, Lenny?'

'Sure.'

'Read it back to me.'

I worked in a diner three years, once. I could remember anything anybody told me – I didn't care how complicated – and rattle it off right back to him. It's a trick; you wipe your mind clean, open your ears, and in it comes: 'Two grilled cheese to go; bacon and tomato, white toast, no mayonnaise. Three coffees; one black, no sugar; one light and sweet; one regular.' You open your mouth, turn toward the sandwich man, and out it comes: 'G.A.C. on two, seaboard. B.T. down, hold the mayo.' You turn toward the coffee cups and put out your hands. Your fingers grab the cups, and you move to the spigot on the urn. You tap the milk jug handle three times over one cup, twice over the other. The third cup slides automatically. The important part of your mind is a million miles away. You put the coffees down, and your mind wipes out that part of the order. The sandwich man hands you two waxpaper-wrapped squares and a plate with the B.T. on it. You give them to the customers, and your mind wipes out the rest of it. It's gone, used up, and all the time the important part of your mind is a million miles away.

I listened to the rigs going up a hill in compound. Pittsburgh, Scranton, Philadelphia . . . Washington, Baltimore, Camden, Newark . . . A diesel went by – a flatbed, with I beams for a load – while I was reading back the last part of what he'd told me.

'That's right, Lenny. That's *right!*'

I suppose it was. In a diner, you eat the orders you foul up.

'Any more tonight?' I asked him.

'No. No, that's enough. I'm going to get some rest, now. Go back to sleep now. Thanks.'

'Sure.'

'No, don't be so casual. You're doing a big thing for me. It's important to me to pass these things on to you people. I'm not going to last much longer.'

'Sure, you are.'

'No, Lennie.'

'Come on.'

'No. I was burning as I fell. Remember the alternate radical in the equation I gave you the first night? The field was distorted by the Sun, and the generator restructured the . . .' He went on, but I don't remember it. I would have had to remember the original equation for it to make any sense to me, and even if I remembered it I would have had to understand it. This business of reading his equations back to him, see . . . that was a trick. Who wants to remember how many grilled cheese sandwiches to go did you sell during the day? I had a wise guy order in double talk, once. I read it back to him like a man running a strip of tape through a recorder, and I wasn't even listening.

'. . . So, you see, Lenny, I'm not going to live. A man in my condition wouldn't survive even in my time and place.'

'You're wrong, Buddy. They'll pull you through. They know their business in this place.'

'Do you really think so, Lenny?' He whispered it with a sad laugh, if you know what I mean.

'Sure,' I said. I was listening to a tanker going by from the north. I could hear the clink of the static chain.

They had brought the man in the next bed in from what they figured was a real bad private plane fire. They said some farmer had seen him falling free, as if he'd jumped without a parachute. They hadn't been able to identify him yet, or find his plane, and he wouldn't give a name. The first two nights he hadn't said a word, until suddenly he said: 'Is anybody listening? Is there someone there?'

I had spoken up, and he had asked me about myself – what my name was, what my trouble was. He wanted to know the name of the town, and the nation, and the date – day, month, and year. I told him. I'd seen him in his bandages, during the day, and a man in shape like that, you don't argue about his questions. You answer him. You're glad for the chance to do him a kindness.

He was a smart man, too. He spoke a mess of languages besides English. He tried me in Hungarian for a while, but he knew it a lot better than I did. It's been a long time since I left the folks in Chicago.

I told the nurse, the next day, that he'd been talking to me. The doctors tried to find out who he was and where from, but he didn't talk to them. He convinced them, I think, that he was back in a coma again; they hadn't much believed me when I said he'd talked sensibly at all. After that, I knew better than to tell anybody anything. If he wanted it his way, he was entitled. Except he found out, like I've said, that if he made a sound during the day, they'd give him another needle. You couldn't blame them. It was their way of doing him a kindness.

I lay back, and watched the ceiling begin getting light from
the first touch of day outside the windows. Traffic was
picking up outside, now. The rigs went by one after another. Farm produce, most likely, catching the market.
Lettuce and potatoes, oranges and onions – I could hear
the crates shifting on top of each other on the big stake
bodies, and the creak of the tie ropes.

'Lenny!'

I answered right away.

'Lenny, the equation for coordinating spacetime is . . .'
He was in a hurry.

'Yeah.' I let it soak into the trick sponge in my mind, and
when he asked me to read it back, I squeezed it dry again.

'Thank you, Lenny,' he said. I could barely hear him –
I began thumping the night-call bell on the cord draped
over the head of my bed.

The next day, there was a new man in the next bed. He
was a hunter – a young fellow, from New York – and he'd
put a load of birdshot all through his right thigh. It was a
couple of days before he wanted to talk, and I didn't get
to know him, much.

I guess it was the second or third afternoon after the new
man had come in, when my doctor straightened up and
pulled the sheet back over my stumps. He looked at me in
a peculiar way, and said, offhandedly: 'Tell you what,
Lenny – suppose we send you down to surgery and take a
little bit more off each of those, hmm?'

'Nuts, Doc, I can smell it, too. Why bother?'

We didn't have much more to say to each other. I lay
thinking about Peoria, Illinois, which used to be more fun
than it has been lately – for truckers, I mean – and St
Louis, and Corpus Christi. I wasn't satisfied with just the
Eastern Seaboard anymore. Sacramento, Seattle, Fairbanks
and that miserable long run over the Alcan Highway . . .

In the middle of the night, I was still remembering. I
could hear the rigs out on the street, but I was really listening to the sound a Cummins makes going into one of those
long switchback grades over the Rockies, and suddenly I

turned my head and whispered: 'Fellow! Hey, fellow – you awake?' to the new man in the next bed.

I heard him grunt. 'What?' He sounded annoyed. But he was listening.

'You ever do any driving? I mean, you ever go down through New Jersey in your car? Well, look, if you ever need a break on tires or a battery, you stop by Jeffrey's Friendly Gas and Oil, on Route 22 in Darlington, and tell 'em Lenny Kovacs sent you. Only watch out – there's a speed trap right outside town, in summer . . . And if you want a good meal, try the Strand Restaurant, down the street there. Or if you're going the other way, up into New England, you take the Boston Post Road and stop by . . . Fellow? You listening?'

Never Meet Again

The breeze soughed through the linden trees. It was warm and gentle as it drifted along the boulevard. It tugged at the dresses of the girls strolling with their young men and stirred their modishly cut hair. It set the banners atop the government buildings to flapping, and it brought with it the sound of a jet aircraft – a Heinkel or a Messerschmitt – rising into the sky from Tempelhof Aerodrome. But when it touched Professor Kempfer on his bench it brought only the scent of the Parisian perfumes and the sight of gaily colored frocks swaying around the girls' long, healthy legs.

Doctor Professor Kempfer straightened his exhausted shoulders and raised his heavy head. His deep, strained eyes struggled to break through their now habitual dull stare.

It was spring again, he realized in faint surprise. The pretty girls were eating their lunches hastily once more, so that they and their young men could stroll along Unter Den Linden, and the young men in the broad-shouldered jackets were clear-eyed and full of their own awakening strength.

And of course Professor Kempfer wore no overcoat today. He was not quite the comic pedant who wore his galoshes in the sunshine. It was only that he had forgotten, for the moment. The strain of these last few days had been very great.

All these months – these years – he had been doing his government-subsidized research and the other thing, too. Four or five hours for the government, and then a full day on the much more important thing no one knew about. Twelve, sixteen hours a day. Home to his very nice government apartment, where Frau Ritter, the housekeeper, had his supper ready. The supper eaten, to bed. And in the morning; cocoa, a bit of pastry, and to work. At noon he would leave his laboratory for a little while, to come here and eat the slice of black bread and cheese Frau Ritter had wrapped in waxed paper and put in his pocket before he left the house.

But it was over, now. Not the government sinecure – that just made work for the old savant who, after all, held the Knight's Cross of the Iron Cross for his work with the anti-submarine radar detector. That, of course, had been fifteen years ago. If they could not quite pension him off, still no one expected anything of a feeble old man puttering around the apparatus they had given him to play with.

And they were right, of course. Nothing *would* ever come of it. But the other thing . . .

That was done, now. After this last little rest he would go back to his laboratory in the Himmlerstrasse and take the final step. So now he could let himself relax and feel the warmth of the sun.

Professor Kempfer smiled wearily at the sunshine. The good, constant sun, he thought, that gives of itself to all of us, no matter who or where we are. Spring . . . April, 1958.

Had it really been fifteen years – and sixteen years since the end of the war? It didn't seem possible. But then one day had been exactly like another for him, with only an electric light in the basement where his real apparatus was, an electric light that never told him whether it was morning, noon, or night.

I have become a cave-dweller! he thought with sudden realization. I have forgotten to think in terms of serial time. What an odd little trick I have played on myself!

Had he *really* been coming here, to this bench, every clear day for *fifteen* years? Impossible! But . . .

He counted on his fingers. 1940 was the year England had surrendered, with its air force destroyed and the Luftwaffe flying unchallenged air cover for the swift invasion. He had been sent to England late that year, to supervise the shipment home of the ultra-short-wave radar from the

Royal Navy's anti-submarine warfare school. And 1941 was the year the U-boats took firm control of the Atlantic. 1942 was the year the Russians lost at Stalingrad, starved by the millions, and surrendered to a Wehrmacht fed on shiploads of Argentinian beef. 1942 was the end of the war, yes.

So it *had* been that long.

I have become an indrawn old man, he thought to himself in bemusement. So very busy with myself . . . and the world has gone by, even while I sat here and might have watched it, if I'd taken the trouble. The world . . .

He took the sandwich from his coat pocket, unwrapped it, and began to eat. But after the first few bites he forgot it, and held it in one hand while he stared sightlessly in front of him.

His pale, mobile lips fell into a wry smile. The world – the vigorous young world, so full of strength, so confident . . . while I worked in my cellar like some Bolshevik dreaming of a fantastic bomb that would wipe out all my enemies at a stroke.

But what I have is not a bomb, and I have no enemies. I am an honored citizen of the greatest empire the world has ever known. Hitler is thirteen years dead in his auto accident, and the new chancellor is a different sort of man. He has promised us no war with the Americans. We have peace, and triumph, and these create a different sort of atmosphere than do war and desperation. We have relaxed, now. We have the fruit of our victory – what do we not have, in our empire of a thousand years? Western civilization is safe at last from the hordes of the East. Our future is assured. There is nothing, no one to fight, and these young people walking here have never known a moment's doubt, an instant's question of their place in an endlessly bright tomorrow. I will soon die, and the rest of us who knew the old days will die soon enough. It will all belong to the young people – all this eternal world. It belongs to them already. It is just that some of us old ones have not yet gotten altogether out of the way.

He stared out at the strolling crowds. How many years

can I possibly have left to me? Three? Two? Four? I could die tomorrow.

He sat absolutely still for a moment, listening to the thick old blood slurring through his veins, to the thready flutter of his heart. It hurt his eyes to see. It hurt his throat to breathe. The skin of his hands was like spotted old paper.

Fifteen years of work. Fifteen years in his cellar, building what he had built – for what? Was his apparatus going to change anything? Would it detract even one trifle from this empire? Would it alter the life of even one citizen in that golden tomorrow?

This would go on exactly as it was. Nothing would change in the least. So, what had he worked for? For himself? For this outworn husk of one man?

Seen in that light, he looked like a very stupid man. Stupid, foolish – monomaniacal.

Dear God, he thought with a rush of terrible intensity, am I now going to persuade myself not to use what I have built?

For all these years he had worked, worked – without stopping, without thinking. Now, in this first hour of rest, was he suddenly going to spit on it all?

A stout bulk settled on the bench beside him. 'Joachim,' the complacent voice said.

Professor Kempfer looked up. 'Ah, Georg!' he said with an embarrassed laugh, 'You startled me.'

Doctor Professor Georg Tanzler guffawed heartily. 'Oh, Jochim, Jochim!' he chuckled, shaking his head. 'What a type you are! A thousand times I've found you here at noon, and each time it seems as if it surprises you. What do you think about, here on your bench?'

Professor Kempfer let his eyes stray. 'Oh, I don't know,' he said gently. 'I look at the young people.'

'The girls — ' Tanzler's elbow dug roguishly into his side. 'The girls, eh, Jochim?'

A veil drew over Professor Kempfer's eyes. 'No,' he whispered. 'Not like that. No.'

'What then?'

'Nothing,' Professor Kempfer said dully. 'I look at nothing.'

Tanzler's mood changed instantly. 'So,' he declared with precision. 'I thought as much. Everyone knows you are working night and day, even though there is no need for it.' Tanzler resurrected a chuckle. 'We are not in any great hurry now. It's not as if we were pressed by anyone. The Australians and Canadians are fenced off by our navy. The Americans have their hands full in Asia. And your project, whatever it may be, will help no one if you kill yourself with overwork.'

'You know there is no project,' Professor Kempfer whispered. 'You know it is all just busy work. No one reads my reports. No one checks my results. They give me the equipment I ask for, and do not mind, as long as it is not too much. You know that quite well. Why pretend otherwise?'

Tanzler sucked his lips. Then he shrugged. 'Well, if you realize, then you realize,' he said cheerfully. Then he changed expression again, and laid his hand on Professor Kempfer's arm in comradely fashion. 'Jochim. It has been fifteen years. Must you still try to bury yourself?'

Sixteen, Professor Kempfer corrected, and then realized Tanzler was not thinking of the end of the war. Sixteen years since then, yes, but fifteen since Marthe died. Only fifteen?

I *must* learn to think in terms of serial time again. He realized Tanzler was waiting for a response, and mustered a shrug.

'Jochim! Have you been listening to me?'

'Listening? Of course, Georg.'

'Of course!' Tanzler snorted, his moustaches fluttering. 'Jochim,' he said positively, 'it is not as if we were young men, I admit. But life goes on, even for us old crocks.' Tanzler was a good five years Kempfer's junior. 'We must look ahead – we must live for a future. We cannot let ourselves sink into the past. I realize you were very fond of Marthe. Every man is fond of his wife – that goes without saying. But fifteen years, Jochim! Surely, it is proper to grieve. But to *mourn*, like this – this is not *healthy!*'

One bright spark singed through the quiet barriers Professor Kempfer had thought perfect. 'Were *you* ever in a camp, Georg?' he demanded, shaking with pent-up violence.

'A camp?' Tanzler was taken aback. 'I? Of course not, Jochim! But – you and Marthe were not in a real *lager* – it was just a . . . a . . . Well, you were under the State's protection! After all, Jochim!'

Professor Kempfer said stubbornly: 'But Marthe *died*. Under the State's protection.'

'These things *happen*, Jochim! After all, you're a reasonable man – Marthe – tuberculosis – even sulfa has its limitations – that might have happened to *anyone!*'

'She did not have tuberculosis in 1939, when we were placed under the State's protection. And when I finally said yes, I would go to work for them, and they gave me the radar detector to work on, they promised me it was only a little congestion in her bronchiae and that as soon as she was well they would bring her home. And the war ended, and they did *not* bring her home. I was given the Knight's Cross from Hitler's hands, personally, but they did *not* bring her home. And the last time I went to the sanitarium to see her, she was *dead*. And they paid for it all, and gave me my laboratory here, and an apartment, and clothes, and food, and a very good housekeeper, but Marthe was *dead*.'

'Fifteen *years*, Jochim! Have you not forgiven us?'

'No. For a little while today – just a little while ago – I thought I might. But – no.'

Tanzler puffed out his lips and fluttered them with an exhaled breath. 'So,' he said. 'What are you going to do to us for it?'

Professor Kempfer shook his head. 'To you? What should I do to you? The men who arranged these things are all dead, or dying. If I had some means of hurting the Reich – and I do not – how could I revenge myself on these children?' He looked toward the passersby. 'What am I to them, or they to me? No – no, I am going to do nothing to you.'

Tanzler raised his eyebrows and put his thick fingertips together. 'If you are going to do nothing to us, then what are you going to do to yourself?'

'I am going to go away.' Already, Professor Kempfer was ashamed of his outburst. He felt he had controverted his essential character. Man of science, after all – a thinking, *reasoning* man – could not let himself descend to emotional levels. Professor Kempfer was embarrassed to think that Tanzler might believe this sort of lapse was typical of him.

'Who am I,' he tried to explain, 'to be judge and jury over a whole nation – an empire? Who is one man, to decide good and evil? I look at these youngsters, and I envy them with all my heart. To be young; to find all the world arranged in orderly fashion for one's special benefit; to have been placed on a surfboard, free to ride the crest of the wave forever, and never to have to swim at all! Who am I, Georg? Who am I?

'But I do not like it here. So I am going away.'

Tanzler looked at him enigmatically. 'To Carlsbad. For the radium waters. Very healthful. We'll go together.' He began pawing Professor Kempfer's arm with great heartiness. 'A splendid idea! I'll get the seats reserved on the morning train. We'll have a holiday, eh, Jochim?'

'No!' He struggled to his feet, pulling Tanzler's hand away from his arm. '*No!*' He staggered when Tanzler gave way. He began to walk fast, faster than he had walked in years. He looked over his shoulder, and saw Tanzler lumbering after him.

He began to run. He raised an arm. 'Taxi! *Taxi!*' He lurched toward the curb, while the strolling young people looked at him wide-eyed.

He hurried through the ground floor laboratory, his heart pumping wildly. His eyes were fixed on the plain gray door to the fire stairs, and he fumbled in his trousers pocket for the key. He stumbled against a bench and sent apparatus crashing over. At the door, he steadied himself and, using both hands, slipped the key into the lock. Once through the door, he slammed it shut and locked it again, and listened to the hoarse whistle of his breath in his nostrils.

Then, down the fire stairs he clattered, open-mouthed. Tanzler. Tanzler would be at a telephone, somewhere. Perhaps the State Police were out in the streets, in their cars, coming here, already.

He wrenched open the basement door, and locked it behind him in the darkness before he turned on the lights. With his chest aching, he braced himself on widespread feet and looked at the dull sheen of yellow light on the racks of gray metal cabinets. They rose about him like the blocks of a Mayan temple, with dials for carvings and pilot lights for jewels, and he moved down the narrow aisle between them, slowly and quietly now, like a last, enfeebled acolyte. As he walked he threw switches, and the cabinets began to resonate in chorus.

The aisle led him, irrevocably, to the focal point. He read what the dials on the master panel told him, and watched the power demand meter inch into the green.

If they think to open the building circuit breakers!

If they shoot through the door!

If I was wrong!

Now there were people hammering on the door. Desperately weary, he depressed the firing switch.

There was a galvanic thrum, half pain, half pleasure, as the vibratory rate of his body's atoms was changed by an infinitesimal degree. Then he stood in dank darkness, breathing musty air, while whatever parts of his equipment had been included in the field fell to the floor.

Behind him, he left nothing. Vital resistors had, by design, come with him. The overloaded apparatus in the basement laboratory began to stench and burn under the surge of full power, and to sputter in Georg Tanzler's face.

The basement he was in was not identical with the one he had left. That could only mean that in this Berlin, something serious had happened to at least one building on the Himmlerstrasse. Professor Kempfer searched through the darkness with weary patience until he found a door, and while he searched he considered the thought that some upheaval, man-made or natural, had filled in the ground for dozens of meters above his head, leaving only this one pocket of emptiness into which his apparatus had shunted him.

When he finally found the door he leaned against it for some time, and then he gently eased it open. There was nothing but blackness on the other side, and at his first step he tripped and sprawled on a narrow flight of stairs, bruising a hip badly. He found his footing again. On quivering legs he climbed slowly and as silently as he could, clinging to the harsh, newly-sawed wood of the bannister. He could not seem to catch his breath. He had to gulp for air, and the darkness was shot through with red swirlings.

He reached the top of the stairs, and another door. There was harsh gray light seeping around it, and he listened intently, allowing for the quick suck and thud of the pulse in his ears. When he heard nothing for a long time, he opened it. He was at the end of a long corridor lined with doors, and at the end there was another door opening on the street.

Eager to get out of the building, and yet reluctant to leave as much as he knew of this world, he moved down the corridor with exaggerated caution.

It was a shoddy building. The paint on the walls was cheap, and the linoleum on the floor was scuffed and warped. There were cracks in the plastering. Everything was rough – half finished, with paint slapped over it, everything drab. There were numbers on the doors, and dirty rope mats in front of them. It was an apartment house, then – but from the way the doors were jammed almost against each other, the apartments had to be no more than cubicles.

Dreary, he thought. Dreary, dreary – who would live in such a place? Who would put up an apartment house for people of mediocre means in this neighbourhood?

But when he reached the street, he saw that it was humpy and cobblestoned, the cobbling badly patched, and that all the buildings were like this one – gray-faced, hulking, ugly. There was not a building he recognized – not a stick or stone of the Himmlerstrasse with its fresh cement roadway and its sapling trees growing along the sidewalk. And yet he knew he must be on the exact spot where the Himmler-strasse had been – was – and he could not quite understand.

He began to walk in the direction of Unter Den Linden. He was far from sure he could reach it on foot, in his con-dition, but he would pass through the most familiar parts of the city, and could perhaps get some inkling of what had happened.

He had suspected that the probability world his apparatus could more easily adjust him for would be one in which Germany had lost the war. That was a large, dramatic difference, and though he had refined his work as well as he could, any first model of any equipment was bound to be relatively insensitive.

But as he walked along, he found himself chilled and repelled by what he saw.

Nothing was the same. Nothing. Even the layout of the streets had changed a little. There were new buildings everywhere – new buildings of a style and workmanship that had made them old in atmosphere the day they were completed. It was the kind of total reconstruction that he had no doubt the builders stubbornly proclaimed was 'Good as New', because to say it was as good as the old Berlin would have been to invite bitter smiles.

The people in the streets were grim, gray-faced, and shoddy. They stared blankly at him and his suit, and once a dumpy woman carrying a string bag full of lumpy pack-ages turned to her similar companion and muttered as he passed that he looked like an American with his extrava-gant clothes.

The phrase frightened him. What kind of war had it been, that there would still be Americans to be hated in Berlin in 1958? How long could it possibly have lasted, to account for so many old buildings gone? What had pounded Germany so cruelly? And yet even the 'new'

51

buildings were genuinely some years old. Why an American? Why not an Englishman or Frenchman?

He walked the gray streets, looking with a numb sense of settling shock at this grim Berlin. He saw men in shapeless uniform caps, brown trousers, cheap boots and sleazy blue shirts. They wore armbands with *Volkspolizei* printed on them. Some of them had not bothered to shave this morning or to dress in fresh uniforms. The civilians looked at them sidelong and then pretended not to have seen them. For an undefinable but well-remembered reason, Professor Kempfer slipped by them as inconspicuously as possible.

He grappled at what he saw with the dulled resources of his overtired intellect, but there was no point of reference with which to begin. He even wondered if perhaps the war was somehow still being fought, with unimaginable alliances and unthinkable antagonists, with all resources thrown into a brutal, dogged struggle from which all hope of both defeat and victory were gone, and only endless straining effort loomed up from the future.

Then he turned the corner and saw the stubby military car, and soldiers in baggy uniforms with red stars on their caps. They were parked under a weatherbeaten sign which read, in German above a few lines in unreadable Cyrillic characters: *Attention! You Are Leaving the U.S.S.R. Zone of Occupation. You Are Entering the American Zone of Occupation. Show Your Papers.*

God in heaven! he thought, recoiling. The Bolsheviks. And he was on their side of the line. He turned abruptly, but did not move for an instant. The skin of his face felt tight. Then he broke into a stumbling walk, back the way he had come.

He had not come into this world blindly. He had not dared bring any goods from his apartment, of course. Not with Frau Ritter to observe him. Nor had he expected that his Reichsmarks would be of any use. He had provided for this by wearing two diamond-set rings. He had expected to have to walk down to the jewellery district before he could begin to settle into this world, but he had expected no further difficulty.

He had expected Germany to have lost the war. Germany had lost another war within his lifetime, and fifteen years later it would have taken intense study for a man in his present position to detect it.

Professor Kempfer had thought it out, slowly, systematically. He had not thought that a Soviet checkpoint might lie between him and the jewellery district.

It was growing cold, as the afternoon settled down. It had not been as warm a day to begin with, he suspected, as it had been in his Berlin. He wondered how it might be, that Germany's losing a war could change the weather, but the important thing was that he was shivering. He was beginning to attract attention not only for his suit but for his lack of a coat.

He had now no place to go, no place to stay the night, no way of getting food. He had no papers, and no knowledge of where to get them or what sort of maneuver would be required to keep him safe from arrest. If anything could save him from arrest. By Russians.

Professor Kempfer began to walk with dragging steps, his body sagging and numb. More and more of the passersby were looking at him sharply. They might well have an instinct for a hunted man. He did not dare look at the occasional policeman.

He was an old man. He had run today, and shaken with nervous anticipation, and finished fifteen years' work, and it had all been a nightmarish error. He felt his heart begin to beat unnaturally in his ears, and he felt a leaping flutter begin in his chest. He stopped, and swayed, and then he forced himself to cross the sidewalk so he could lean against a building. He braced his back and bent his knees a little, and let his hands dangle at his sides.

The thought came to him that there was an escape for him into one more world. His shoulder-blades scraped a few centimeters downward against the wall.

There were people watching him. They ringed him in at a distance of about two meters, looking at him with almost childish curiosity. But there was something about them that made Professor Kempfer wonder at the conditions that could produce such children. As he looked back at them, he thought that perhaps they all wanted to help him – that would account for their not going on about their business. But they did not know what sort of complications their help might bring to them – except that there would certainly be complications. So none of them approached him. They gathered around him, watching, in a crowd that would momentarily attract a *volkspolizier*.

He looked at them dumbly, breathing as well as he could, his palms flat against the wall. There were stocky old women, round-shouldered men, younger men with pinched faces, and young girls with an incalculable wisdom in their eyes. And there was a bird-like older woman, coming quickly along the sidewalk, glancing at him curiously, then hurrying by, skirting around the crowd . . .

There was one possibility of his escape to this world that Professor Kempfer had not allowed himself to consider. He pushed himself away from the wall, scattering the crowd as though by physical force, and lurched toward the passing woman.

'Marthe!'

She whirled, her purse flying to the ground. Her hand went to her mouth. She whispered, through her knuckles: 'Jochim . . . Jochim . . .' He clutched her, and they supported each other. 'Jochim . . . the American bombers killed you in Hamburg . . . yesterday I sent money to put flowers on your grave . . . Jochim . . .'

'It was a mistake. It was all a mistake. Marthe . . . we have found each other . . .'

From a distance, she had not changed very much at all. Watching her move about the room as he lay, warm and clean, terribly tired, in her bed, he thought to himself that she had not aged half as much as he. But when she bent over him with the cup of hot soup in her hand, he saw the sharp lines in her face, around her eyes and mouth, and when she spoke he heard the dry note in her voice.

How many years? he thought. How many years of loneliness and grief? *When* had the Americans bombed Hamburg? How? What kind of aircraft could bomb Germany from bases in the Western Hemisphere?

They had so much to explain to each other. As she worked to make him comfortable, the questions flew between them.

'It was something I stumbled on. The theory of probability worlds – of alternate universes. Assuming that the characteristic would be a difference in atomic vibration – minute, you understand; almost infinitely minute – assuming that somewhere in the gross universe every possible variation of every event *must* take place – then if some means could be found to alter the vibratory rate within a field, then any object in that field would automatically become part of the universe corresponding to that vibratory rate . . .

'Marthe, I can bore you later. Tell me about *Hamburg*. Tell me how we lost the war. Tell me about Berlin.'

He listened while she told him how their enemies had ringed them in – how the great white wastes of Russia had swallowed their men, and the British fire bombers had murdered children in the night. How the Wehrmacht fought, and fought, and smashed their enemies back time after time, until all the best soldiers were dead. And how the Americans with their dollars, had poured out countless tons of equipment to make up for their inability to fight. How, at the last, the vulture fleets of bombers had rumbled inexhaustibly across the sky, killing, killing, killing, until all the German homes and German families had been destroyed. And how now the Americans, with their hellish bomb that had killed a hundred thousand Japanese civilians, now bestrode the world and tried to bully it, with their bombs and their dollars, into final submission.

How? Professor Kempfer thought. How could such a thing have happened?

Slowly, he pieced it together, mortified to find himself annoyed when Marthe interrupted with constant questions about his Berlin and especially about his equipment.

And, pieced together, it still refused to seem logical.

How could anyone believe that Goering, in the face of all good sense, would turn the Luftwaffe from destroying the R.A.F. bases to a ridiculous attack on English cities? How could anyone believe that German electronics scientists could persistently refuse to believe ultra-short-wave radar was practical – refuse to believe it even when the Allied hunter planes were finding surfaced submarines at night with terrible accuracy?

What kind of nightmare world was this, with Germany divided and the Russians in control of Europe, in control of Asia, reaching for the Middle East that no Russian, not even the dreaming czars, had seriously expected ever to attain?

'Marthe – we must get out of this place. We must. I will have to rebuild my machine.' It would be incredibly difficult. Working clandestinely as he must, scraping components together – even now that the work had been done once, it would take several years.

Professor Kempfer looked inside himself to find the strength he would need. And it was not there. It simply was gone, used up, burnt out, eaten out.

'Marthe, you will have to help me. I must take some of your strength. I will need so many things – identity papers, some kind of work so we can eat, money to buy equipment . . .' His voice trailed away. It was so much, and there was so little time left for him. Yet, somehow, they must do it.

A hopelessness, a feeling of inevitable defeat, came over him. It was this world. It was poisoning him.

Marthe's hand touched his brow. 'Hush, Jochim. Go to sleep. Don't worry. Everything is all right, now. My poor Jochim, how terrible you look! But everything will be all right. I must go back to work, now. I am hours late already. I will come back as soon as I can. Go to sleep, Jochim.'

He let his breath out in a long, tired sigh. He reached up and touched her hand. 'Marthe . . .'

He awoke to Marthe's soft urging. Before he opened his eyes he had taken her hand from his shoulder and clasped it tightly. Marthe let the contact linger for a moment, then broke it gently.

'Jochim – my superior at the Ministry is here to see you.'

He opened his eyes and sat up. 'Who?'

'Colonel Lubintsev, from the People's Government Ministerium, where I work. He would like to speak to you.' She touched him reassuringly. 'Don't worry. It's all right. I spoke to him – I explained. He's not here to arrest you. He's waiting in the other room.'

He looked at Marthe dumbly. 'I – I must get dressed,' he managed to say after a while.

'No – no, he wants you to stay in bed. He knows you're exhausted. He asked me to assure you it would be all right. Rest in bed. I'll get him.'

Professor Kempfer sank back. He looked unseeingly up at the ceiling until he heard the sound of a chair being drawn up beside him, and then he slowly turned his head.

Colonel Lubintsev was a stocky, ruddy-faced man with gray bristles on his scalp. He had an astonishingly boyish smile. 'Doctor Professor Kempfer, I am honored to meet you,' he said. 'Lubinstev, Colonel, assigned as advisor to the People's Government Ministerium.' He extended his hand gravely, and Professor Kempfer shook it with a conscious effort.

'I am pleased to make your acquaintance,' Professor Kempfer mumbled.

'Not at all, Doctor Professor. Not at all. Do you mind if I smoke?'

'Please.' He watched the colonel touch a lighter to a long cigarette while Marthe quickly found a saucer for an ashtray. The colonel nodded his thanks to Marthe, puffed on the cigarette, and addressed himself to Professor Kempfer while Marthe sat down on a chair against the far wall.

'I have inspected your dossier,' Colonel Lubintsev said. 'That is,' with a smile, 'our dossier on your late counterpart. I see you fit the photographs as well as could be expected. We will have to make a further identification, of course, but I rather think that will be a formality.' He smiled again. 'I am fully prepared to accept your story. It is too fantastic not to be true. Of course, sometimes foreign agents choose their cover stories with that idea in mind, but not in this case, I think. If what has happened to you could happen to any man, our dossier indicates Jochim Kempfer might well be that man.' Again, the smile. 'In any counterpart.'

'You have a dossier,' Professor Kempfer said.

Colonel Lubintsev's eyebrows went up in a pleased grin. 'Oh, yes. When we liberated your nation, we knew exactly what scientists were deserving of our assistance in their work, and where to find them. We had laboratories, project agendas, living quarters – everything! – all ready for them. But I must admit, we did not think we would ever be able to accommodate you.'

'But now you can.'

'Yes!' Once more, Colonel Lubintsev smiled like a little boy with great fun in store. 'The possibilities of your device are as infinite as the universe! Think of the enormous help to the people of your nation, for example, if they could draw on machine tools and equipment from such alternate places as the one you have just left.' Colonel Lubintsev waved his cigarette. 'Or if, when the Americans attack us, we can transport bombs from a world where the revolution is an accomplished fact, and have them appear in North America in this.'

Professor Kempfer sat up in bed. 'Marthe! Marthe, why have you done this to me?'

'Hush, Jochim,' she said. 'Please. Don't tire yourself. I have done nothing to you. You will have care, now. We will be able to live together in a nice villa, and you will be able to work, and we will be together.'

'Marthe— '

She shook her head, her lips pursed primly. 'Please, Jochim. Times have changed a great deal, here. I explained to the Colonel that your head was probably still full of the old Nazi propaganda. He understands. You will learn to see it for what it was. And you will help put the Americans back in their place.' Her eyes filled suddenly with tears.

58

'All the years I went to visit your grave as often as I could. All the years I paid for flowers, and all the nights I cried for you.'

'But I am *here*, Marthe! I am here! I am not dead.'

'Jochim, Jochim,' she said gently. 'Am I to have had all my grief for nothing?'

'I have brought a technical expert with me,' Colonel Lubintsev went on as though nothing had happened. 'If you will tell him what facilities you will need, we can begin preliminary work immediately.' He rose to his feet. 'I will send him in. I myself must be going.' He put out his cigarette, and extended his hand. 'I have been honoured, Doctor Professor Kempfer.'

'Yes,' Professor Kempfer whispered. 'Yes. Honoured.' He raised his hand, pushed it toward the colonel's, but could not hold it up long enough to reach. It fell back to the coverlet, woodenly, and Professor Kempfer could not find the strength to move it. 'Goodbye.'

He heard the colonel walk out with a few murmured words for Marthe. He was quite tired, and he heard only a sort of hum.

He turned his head when the technical expert came in. The man was all eagerness, all enthusiasm:

'Jochim! This is amazing! Perhaps I should introduce myself – I worked with your counterpart during the war – we were quite good friends – I am Georg Tanzler. Jochim! How *are* you!'

Professor Kempfer looked up. He saw through a deep, tightening fog, and he heard his heart preparing to stop. His lips twisted. 'I think I am going away again, Georg,' he whispered.

The Burning World

I

They walked past rows of abandoned offices in the last government office building in the world – two men who looked vastly different, but who had crucial similarities.

Josef Kimmensen had full lips trained to set in a tight, thin line, and live, intelligent eyes. He was tall and looked thin, though he was not. He was almost sixty years old, and his youth and childhood had been such that now his body was both old for its years and still a compact, tightly-wound mechanism of bone and muscle fiber.

Or had been, until an hour ago. Then it had failed him; and his one thought now was to keep Jem Bendix from finding out how close he was to death.

Jem Bendix was a young man, about twenty-eight, with a broad, friendly grin and a spring to his step. His voice, when he spoke, was low and controlled. He was the man Josef Kimmensen had chosen to replace him as president of the Freemen's League.

The building itself was left over from the old regime. It was perhaps unfortunate – Kimmensen had often debated the question with himself – to risk the associations that clung to the building. But a building is only a building, and the dust of years chokes the past to death. It was better to work here than to build a new set of offices. It might seem a waste to leave a still-new building, and that might tend to make people linger after their jobs had finished themselves. The pile of cracking bricks and peeled marble facings would be falling in a heap soon, and the small staff that still worked here couldn't help but be conscious of it. It was probably a very useful influence.

They walked through the domed rotunda, with its columns, echoing alcoves, and the jag-topped pedestals where the old regime's statues had been sledge-hammered away. The rotunda was gloomy, its skylight buried under rain-borne dust and drifted leaves from the trees on the mountainside. There was water puddled on the rotten marble floor under a place where the skylight's leading was gone.

Kimmensen left the day's letters with the mail clerk, and he and Bendix walked out to the plaza, where his plane was parked. Around the plaza, the undergrowth was creeping closer every year, and vine runners were obscuring the hard precision of the concrete's edge. On all sides, the mountains towered up toward the pale sun, their steep flanks cloaked in snow and thick stands of bluish evergreen. There was a hight breeze in the crystalline air, and a tang of fir sap.

Kimmensen breathed in deeply. He loved these mountains. He had been born in the warm lowlands, where a man's blood did not stir so easily nor surge so strongly through his veins. Even the air here was freedom's air.

As they climbed into his plane, he asked: 'Did anything important come up in your work today, Jem?'

Jem shrugged uncertainly. 'I don't know. Nothing that's urgent at the moment. But it might develop into something. I meant to speak to you about it after dinner. Did Salmaggi tell you one of our families was burned out up near the northwest border?'

Kimmensen shook his head and pressed his lips together. 'No, he didn't. I didn't have time to see him today.' Perhaps he should have. But Salmaggi was the inevitable misfit who somehow creeps into every administrative body. He was a small, fat, tense, shrilly argumentative man who fed on alarms like a sparrow. Somehow, through election after election, he had managed to be returned as Land Use Advisor. Supposedly, his duties were restricted to helping the old agricultural districts convert to synthetic diets. But that limitation had never restrained his busybody nature. Consultations with him were full of sidetracks into politics, alarmisms, and piping declamations about things like the occasional family found burned out.

Kimmensen despaired of ever making the old-fashioned politician types like Salmaggi understand the new society.

61

Kimmensen, too, could feel sorrow at the thought of home-steads razed, of people dead in the midst of what they had worked to build. It was hard – terribly hard – to think of; too easy to imagine each might be his own home. Too easy to come upon the charred embers and feel that a horrible thing had been done, without taking time to think that perhaps this family had abused its freedom. Sentiment was the easy thing. But logic reminded a man that some people were quarrelsome, that some people insisted on living their neighbours' lives, that some people were offensive.

There were people with moral codes they clung to and lived by people who worshipped in what they held to be the only orthodox way, people who clung to some idea – some rock on which their lives rested. Well and good. But if they tried to inflict these reforms on their neighbours, patience could only go so far, and the tolerance of fanaticism last just so long.

Kimmensen sighed as he fumbled with his seat belt buckle, closed the power contacts, and engaged the vanes. 'We're haunted by the past, Jem,' he said tiredly. 'Salmaggi can't keep himself from thinking like a supervisor. He can't learn that quarrels between families are the families' business.' He nodded to himself. 'It's a hard thing to learn, sometimes. But if Salmaggi doesn't, one of these days he may not come back from his hoppings around the area.'

'I wouldn't be worrying, Joe,' Jem said with a nod of agreement. 'But Salmaggi tells me there's a fellow who wants to get a group of men together and take an army into the northwest. This fellow – Anse Messerschmidt's his name – is saying these things are raids by the North-westers.'

'Is he getting much support?' Kimmensen asked quickly.

'I don't know. It doesn't seem likely. After all, the North-westers're people just like us.'

Kimmensen frowned, and for one bad moment he was frightened. He remembered, in his youth – it was only twenty-eight years ago – Bausch strutting before his cheer-ing crowds, bellowing hysterically about the enemies sur-rounding them – the lurking armies of the people to the south, to the east, the northwest; every compass point held enemies for Bausch. Against those enemies, there must be mighty armies raised. Against those enemies, there must be Leadership – firm Leadership: Bausch.

'Armies!' he burst out. 'The day Freemen organize to invade another area is the day they stop being Freemen. They become soldiers, loyal to the army and their generals. They lose their identification with their homes and families. They become a separate class – an armed, organized class of military specialists no one family can stand against. And on that day, freedom dies for everybody.

'You understand me, don't you, Jem? You understand how dangerous talk like this Messerschmidt's can be?' Kimmensen knew Bendix did. But it was doubly important to be doubly assured, just now.

Bendix nodded, his quick, easy smile growing on his face. 'I feel the same way, Joe.' And Kimmensen, looking at him, saw that Jem meant it. He had watched Jem grow up – had worked with him for the past ten years. They thought alike; their logic followed the same, inevitable paths. Kimmensen couldn't remember one instance of their disagreeing on anything.

The plane was high in the air. Below them, green forests filled the valleys, and the snow on the mountaintops was red with the light of sunset. On the east sides of the slopes, twilight cast its shadows. Kimmensen looked down at the plots of open ground, some still in crops, others light green with grass against the dark green of the trees. Off in the far west, the sun was half in the distant ocean, and the last slanting rays of direct light reflected from the snug roofs of houses nestled under trees.

Here is the world, Kimmensen thought. Here is the world we saw in the times before we fought out our freedom. Here is the world Dubrovic gave us, working in the cold of his cellar, looking like a maniac gnome, with his beard and his long hair, putting circuits together by candle-light, coughing blood and starving. Here is the world Anna and I saw together.

That was a long time ago. I was thirty-two, and Anna a

worn thirty, with silver in her fine black hair, before we were free to build the house and marry. In the end, we weren't as lucky as we thought, to have come through the fighting years. The doctors honestly believed they'd gotten all the toxins out of her body, but in the end, she died.

Still, here it is, or almost. It isn't given to very many men to have their dreams come true in their lifetimes.

Kimmensen's house stood on the side of a mountain, with its back to the north and glass walls to catch the sun. There was a patio, and a lawn. Kimmensen had been the first to break away from the old agricultural life in this area. There was no reason why a man couldn't like synthetic foods just as well as the natural varieties. Like so many other things, the clinging to particular combinations of the few basic flavors was a matter of education and nothing else. With Direct Power to transmute chemicals for him, a man was not tied to cows and a plow.

The plane settled down to its stand beside the house, and they got out and crossed the patio. The carefully tended dwarf pines and cedars in their planters were purple silhouettes against the sky. Kimmensen opened the way into the living room, then slid the glass panel back into place behind them.

The living room was shadowy and almost dark, despite the glass. Kimmensen crossed the softly whispering rug. 'Apparently Susanne hasn't come home yet. She told me she was going to a party this afternoon.' He took a deep, unhappy breath. 'Sit down, Jem – I'll get you a drink while we're waiting.' He touched the base of a lamp on an end table, and the room came to life under a soft glow of light. The patio went pitch-black by comparison.

'Scotch and water, Jem?'

Bendix held up a thumb and forefinger pressed together. 'Just a pinch, Joe. A little goes a long way with me, you know.'

Kimmensen nodded and went into the kitchen.

The cookers were glowing in the dark, pilot lights glinting. He touched the wall switch. The light panels came on, and he took glasses out of the cupboard. Splashing water from the ice-water tap, he shook his head with resigned impatience.

Susanne should have been home. Putting the dinner in the cookers and setting the timers was not enough, no matter how good the meal might be – and Susanne was an excellent meal planner. She ought to have been home, waiting to greet them. He wouldn't have minded so much, but she'd known Jem was going to be here. If she had to go to the Ennerth girl's party, she could have come home early. She was insulting Jem.

Kimmensen opened the freezer and dropped ice cubes into the glasses. She never enjoyed herself at parties. She always came home downcast and quiet. Yet she went, grim-faced, determined.

He shook his head again, and started to leave the kitchen He stopped to look inside the cookers, each with its Direct Power unit humming softly, each doing its automatic work perfectly. Once the prepared dishes had been tucked inside and the controls set, they could be left to supervise themselves. One operation followed perfectly upon another, with feedback monitors varying temperatures as a dish began to brown, with thermo-couples and humidity detectors always on guard, built into an exactly balanced system and everything done just right.

He touched the temperature controls, resetting them just a trifle to make sure, and went back out into the living room. He took the bottle of carefully compounded Scotch out of the sideboard, filled two shot glasses, and went over to Bendix.

'Here you are, Jem.' He sat down jerkily, dropping rather than sinking into the chair.

Dying angered him. He felt no slowdown in his mind – his brain, he was sure, could still chew a fact the way it always had. He felt no drying out in his brain cells, no mental sinews turning into brittle cords.

He'd been lucky, yes. Not many men had come whole out of the fighting years. Now his luck had run out, and that was the end of it. There were plenty of good men long in the ground. Now he'd join them, not having done badly.

C

Nothing to be ashamed of, and a number of grounds for quiet pride, if truth be told. Still, it made him angry.

'Susanne ought to be home any moment,' he growled.

Jem smiled. 'Take it easy, Joe. You know how these kids are. She probably has to wait 'til somebody else's ready to leave so she can get a lift home.'

Kimmensen grunted. 'She could have found a way to get home in time. I offered to let her take the plane if she wanted to. But, no, she said she'd get a ride over.'

The puzzled anger he always felt toward Susanne was making his head wag. She'd annoyed him for years about the plane, ever since she was eighteen. Then, when he offered her its occasional use after she'd reached twenty-five, she had made a point of not taking it. He couldn't make head or tail of the girl. She was quick, intelligent, educated – she was potentially everything he'd tried to teach her to be. But she was wilful – stubborn. She refused to listen to his advice. The growing coldness between them left them constantly at swords' points. He wondered sometimes if there hadn't been something hidden in Anna's blood – some faint strain that had come to the surface in Susanne and warped her character.

No matter – she was still his daughter. He'd do his duty toward her.

'This is really very good, Joe,' Jem remarked, sipping his drink. 'Excellent.'

'Thank you,' Kimmensen replied absently. He was glaringly conscious of the break in what should have been a smooth evening's social flow. 'Please accept my apologies for Susanne's thoughtlessness.'

Jem smiled. 'There's nothing to apologize for, Joe. When the time comes for her to settle down, she'll do it.'

'Tell me, Jem — ' Kimmensen started awkwardly. But he had to ask. 'Do you like Susanne? I think you do, but tell me anyhow.'

Jem nodded quietly. 'Very much. She's moody and she's headstrong. But that'll change. When it does, I'll ask her.'

Kimmensen nodded to himself. Once again, his judgment of Bendix was confirmed. Most young people were full of action. Everything had to be done now. They hadn't lived long enough to understand how many tomorrows there were in even the shortest life.

But Jem was different. He was always willing to wait and let things unfold themselves. He was cautious and solemn beyond his years. He'd make Susanne the best possible husband, and an excellent president for the League.

'It's just as well we've got a little time,' Jem was saying. 'I was wondering how much you knew about Anse Messerschmidt.'

Kimmensen frowned. 'Messerschmidt? Nothing. And everything. His kind're all cut out of the same pattern.'

Jem frowned with him. 'I've seen him once or twice. He's about my age, and we've bumped into each other at friends' houses. He's one of those swaggering fellows, always ready to start an argument.'

'He'll start one too many, one day.'

'I hope so.'

Kimmensen grunted, and they relapsed into silence. Nevertheless, he felt a peculiar uneasiness. When he heard the other plane settling down outside his house, he gripped his glass tighter. He locked his eyes on the figure of Susanne walking quickly up to the living room wall, and the lean shadow behind her. Then the panel opened and Susanne and her escort stepped out of the night and into the living room. Kimmensen took a sudden breath. He knew Susanne, and he knew that whatever she did was somehow always the worst possible thing. A deep, pain-ridden shadow crossed his face.

Susanne turned her face to look up at the man standing as quietly as one of Death's outriders behind her.

'Hello, Father,' she said calmly. 'Hello, Jem. I'd like you both to meet Anse Messerschmidt.'

II

It had happened at almost exactly four o'clock that afternoon.

As he did at least once each day, Kimmensen had been checking his Direct Power side-arm. The weapon lay on the desk blotter in front of him. The calloused heel of his right palm held it pressed against the blotter while his forefinger pushed the buttplate aside. He moved the safety slide, pulling the focus grid out of the way, and depressed the squeeze triggers with his index and little fingers, holding the weapon securely in his folded-over palm. Inside the butt, the coil began taking power from the mysterious *somewhere* it was aligned on. Old Dubrovic, with his sheaves of notations and encoded symbology, could have told him. But Dubrovic had been killed in one spiteful last gasp of the old regime, for giving the world as much as he had.

The pea-sized tubes flashed into life. Kimmensen released the triggers, slid the buttplate back, and pushed the safety slide down. The side-arm was working – as capable of leveling a mountain as of burning a thread-thin hole in a man.

He put the side-arm back in its holster. Such was the incarnation of freedom. The side-arm did not need to be machined out of metal, or handgripped in oil-finished walnut. These were luxuries. It needed only a few pieces of wire, twisted just so – it was an easy thing to learn – a few tubes out of an old radio. And from the moment you had one, you were a free man. You were an army to defend your rights. And when everybody had one – when Direct Power accumulators lighted your house, drove your plane, let you create building materials, food, clothing out of any cheap, plentiful substance; when you needed no Ministry of Supply, no Board of Welfare Supervision, no Bureau of Employment Allocation, no Ministry of the Interior, no National Police – when all these things were as they were, then the world was free.

He smiled to himself. Not very many people thought of

it in those technical terms, but it made no difference. They knew how it felt. He remembered talking to an old man, a year after the League was founded.

'Mr Kimmensen, don't talk no Silas McKinley to me. I ain't never read a book in my life. I remember young fellers comin' around to court my daughter. Every once in a while, they'd get to talkin' politics with me – I gotta admit, my daughter wasn't so much. They'd try and explain about Fascism and Bureaucracy and stuff like that, and they used to get pretty worked up, throwin' those big words around. All I knew was, the government fellers used to come around and take half of my stuff for taxes. One of 'em finally come around and took my daughter. And I couldn't do nothin' about it. I used to have to work sixteen hours a day just to eat.

'O.K., so now you come around and try and use your kind of big words on me. All I know is, I got me a house, I got me some land, and I got me a wife and some new daughters. And I got me a gun, and ain't nobody gonna take any of 'em away from me.' The old man grinned and patted the weapon at his waist. 'So, if it's all the same to you, I'll just say anything you say is O.K. by me long's it adds up to me bein' my own boss.'

That had been a generation ago. But Kimmensen still remembered it as the best possible proof of the freedom he believed in. He had paid great prices for it in the past. Now that the old regime was as dead as most of the men who remembered it, he would still have been instantly ready to pay them again.

But no one demanded those sacrifices. Twenty-eight years had passed, as uneventful and unbrokenly routine as the first thirty years of his life had been desperate and dangerous. Even the last few traces of administration he represented would soon have withered away, and then his world would be complete. He reached for the next paper in his IN basket.

He felt the thready flutter in his chest and stiffened with surprise. He gripped the edge of his desk, shocked at the way this thing was suddenly upon him.

A bubble effervesced wildly in the cavity under his ribs, like a liquid turned hot in a flash.

He stared blindly. Here it was, in his fifty-ninth year. The knock on the door. He'd never guessed how it would finally come. It hadn't had to take the form of this terrible bubble. It might as easily have been a sudden sharp burst behind his eyes or a slower, subtler gnawing at his vitals. But he'd known it was coming, as every man knows and tries to forget it is coming.

The searing turbulence mounted into his throat. He opened his mouth, strangling. Sudden cords knotted around his chest and, even strangling, he groaned. *Angina pectoris* – pain in the chest – the second-worst pain a man can feel.

The bubble burst and his jaws snapped shut, his teeth mashing together in his lower lip. He swayed in his chair and thought:

That's it. Now I'm an old man.

After a time, he carefully mopped his lips and chin with a handkerchief and pushed the bloodied piece of cloth into the bottom of his wastebasket, under the crumpled disposal of his day's work. He kept his lips compressed until he was sure the cuts had clotted, and decided that, with care, he could speak and perhaps even eat without their being noticed.

Suddenly, there were many things for him to decide quickly. He glanced at the clock on his desk. In an hour, Jem Bendix would be dropping by from his office down the hall. It'd be time to go home, and tonight Jem was invited to come to dinner.

Kimmensen shook his head. He wished he'd invited Jem for some other day. Then he shrugged, thinking: I'm acting as though the world's changed. It hasn't; I have. Some arrangements will have to change, but they will change for the quicker.

He nodded to himself. He'd wanted Susanne and Jem to meet more often. Just as well he'd made the invitation for tonight. Now, more than ever, that might be the solution to one problem. Susanne was twenty-five now; she couldn't help but be losing some of her callow ideas. Give her a husband's firm hand and steadying influence, a baby or two to occupy her time, and she'd be all right. She'd never be what he'd hoped for in a daughter, but it was too late for any more efforts toward changing that. At least she'd be all right.

He looked at his clock again. Fifty-five minutes. Time slipped away each moment your back was turned.

He hooked his mouth, forgetting the cuts, and winced. He held his palm pressed against his lips and smiled wryly in his mind. Five minutes here, five minutes there, and suddenly twenty-eight years were gone. Twenty-eight years in this office. He never thought it'd take so long to work himself out of a job, and here he wasn't quite finished even yet. When he'd accepted the League presidency, he'd thought he only needed a few years – two or three – before the medical and educational facilities were established well enough to function automatically. Well, they had been. Any League member could go to a hospital or a school and find another League member who'd decided to become a doctor or a teacher.

That much *had* been easy. In some areas, people had learned to expect cooperation from other people, and had stopped expecting some all-powerful Authority to step in and give orders. But then, medicine and education had not quite gotten under the thumb of the State in this part of the world.

The remainder had been hard. He'd expected, in a sort of naïve haze, that everyone could instantly make the transition from the old regime to the new freedom. If he'd had any doubts at all, he'd dismissed them with the thought that this was, after all, mountainous country, and mountaineers were always quick to assert their personal independence. Well, they were. Except for a lingering taint from what was left of the old generation, the youngsters would be taking to freedom as naturally as they drew breath. But it had taken a whole generation. The oldsters still thought of a Leader when they thought of their president. They were accustomed to having an Authority think for them, and they confused the League with a government.

Kimmensen shuffled through the papers on his desk. There they were; requests for food from areas unused to a world where no one issued Agricultural Allocations, letters from people styling themselves Mayors of towns . . . The old fictions died hard. Crazy old Dubrovic had given men everywhere the weapon of freedom, but only time and patience would give them full understanding of what freedom was.

Well, after all, this area had been drowned for centuries in the blood of rebellious men. It was the ones who gave in easily who'd had the leisure to breed children. He imagined things were different in the Western Hemisphere, where history had not had its tyrannous centuries to grind away the spirited men. But even here, more and more families were becoming self-contained units, learning to synthesize food and turn farms into parks, abandoning the marketplace towns that should have died with the first MGB man found burned in an alley.

It was coming – the day when all men would be as free of their past as of their fellow men. It seemed, now, that he would never completely see it. That was too bad. He'd hoped for at least some quiet years at home. But that choice had been made twenty-eight years ago.

Sometimes a man had to be a prisoner of his own conscience. He could have stayed home and let someone else do it, but freedom was too precious to consign to someone he didn't fully trust.

Now he'd have to call a League election as soon as possible. Actually, the snowball was well on its way downhill, and all that remained for the next president was the tying up of some loose ends. The business in the outlying districts – the insistence on mistaking inter-family disputes for raids from the northwest – would blow over. A society of armed Freeman families had to go through such a period. Once mutual respect was established – once the penalty for anti-sociability became quite clear – then the society would function smoothly.

And as for who would succeed him, there wasn't a better candidate than Jem Bendix. Jem had always thought the way he did, and Jem was intelligent. Furthermore, everyone liked Jem – there'd be no trouble about the election.

So that was settled. He looked at his clock again and saw that he had a half hour more. He pushed his work out of the way, reached into a drawer, and took out a few sheets of paper. He frowned with impatience at himself as his hands fumbled. For a moment, he brooded down at the seamed stumps where the old regime's police wires had cut through his thumbs. Then, holding his pen clamped firmly between his middle and index knuckles, he began writing:

'I, Joseph Ferassi Kimmensen, being of sound mind and mature years, do make the following Will . . .'

III

Messerschmidt was tall and bony as a wolfhound. His long face was pale, and his ears were large and prominent. Of his features, the ears were the first to attract a casual glance. Then attention shifted to his mouth, hooked in a permanent sardonic grimace under his blade of a nose. Then his eyes caught, and held. They were dark and set close together, under shaggy black eyebrows. There was something in them that made Kimmensen's hackles rise.

He tried to analyze it as Messerschmidt bowed slightly from the hips, his hands down at the sides of his dark clothes.

'Mr President, I'm honored.'

'Messerschmidt.' Kimmensen acknowledged, out of courtesy. The man turned slightly and bowed to Bendix. 'Mr Secretary.'

And now Kimmensen caught it. Toward him, Messerschmidt had been a bit restrained. But his bow to Jem was a shade too deep, and his voice as he delivered Jem's title was too smooth.

It was mockery. Deep, ineradicable, and unveiled, it lurked in the backs of Messerschmidt's eyes. Mockery –

and the most colossal ego Kimmensen had ever encountered.

Good God! Kimmensen thought, I *believed we'd killed all your kind!*

'Father, I invited —' Susanne had begun, her face animated for once. Now she looked from Jem to Kimmensen and her face fell and set into a mask. 'Never mind,' she said flatly. She looked at Kimmensen again, and turned to Messerschmidt. 'I'm sorry, Anse. You'll excuse me. I have to see to the dinner.'

'Of course, Susanne,' Messerschmidt said. 'I hope to see you again.'

Susanne nodded – a quick, sharp jerk of her head – and went quickly into the kitchen. Messerschmidt, Jem, and Kimmensen faced each other.

'An awkward situation,' Messerschmidt said quietly.

'You made it,' Kimmensen answered.

Messerschmidt shrugged. 'I'll take the blame. I think we'd best say good night.'

'Good night.'

'Good night, Mr President . . . Mr Secretary.'

Messerschmidt bowed to each of them and stepped out of the living room, carefully closing the panel behind him. He walked through the pool of light from the living room and disappeared into the darkness on the other side of the patio. In a minute, Kimmensen heard his plane beat its way into the air, and then he sat down again, clutching his glass. He saw that Bendix was white-lipped and shaking.

'So now I've met him,' Kimmensen said, conscious of the strain in his voice.

'That man can't be allowed to stay alive!' Bendix burst out. 'If all the things I hate were ever personified, they're in him.'

Yes,' Kimmensen said, nodding slowly. 'You're right – he's dangerous.' But Kimmensen was less ready to let his emotions carry him away. The days of political killings were over – finished forever. 'But I think we can trust the society to pull his teeth.'

Kimmensen hunched forward in thought. 'We'll talk

about it tomorrow, at work. Our personal feelings are unimportant, compared to the steps we have to take as League officers.'

That closed the matter for tonight, as he'd hoped it would. He still hoped that somehow tonight's purpose could be salvaged.

In that, he was disappointed. It was an awkward, forced meal, with the three of them silent and pretending nothing had happened, denying the existence · of another human being. They were three people attempting to live in a sharply restricted private universe, their conversation limited to comments on the food. At the end of the evening, all their nerves were screaming. Susanne's face was pinched and drawn together, her temples white. When Kimmensen blotted his lips, he found fresh blood on the napkin.

Jem stood up awkwardly. 'Well . . . thank you very much for inviting me, Joe.' He looked toward Susanne and hesitated. 'It was a delicious meal, Sue. Thank you.'

'You're welcome.'

'Well . . . I'd better be getting home . . .'

Kimmensen nodded, terribly disappointed. He'd planned to let Susanne fly Jem home.

'Take the plane, Jem,' he said finally. 'You can pick me up in the morning.'

'All right. Thank you . . . Good night, Sue.'

'Good night.'

'Joe.'

'Good night, Jem.' He wanted to somehow restore Bendix's spirits. 'We'll have a long talk about that other business in the morning,' he reminded him.

'Yes, sir.' It did seem to raise his chin a little.

After Jem had left, Kimmensen turned slowly toward Susanne. She sat quietly, her eyes on her empty coffee cup.

Waiting, Kimmensen thought.

She knew, of course, that she'd hurt him badly again. She expected his anger. Well, how could he help but be angry? Hadn't any of the things he'd told her ever made any impression on her?

'Susanne.'

She raised her head and he saw the stubborn, angry set to her mouth. 'Father, please don't lecture me again.' Every word was low, tight, and controlled.

Kimmensen clenched his hands. He'd never been able to understand this kind of defiance. Where did she get that terribly misplaced hardness in her fiber? What made her so unwilling to listen when someone older and wiser tried to teach her?

If I didn't love her, he thought, this wouldn't matter to me. But in spite of everything, I do love her. So I go on, every day, trying to make her see.

'I can't understand you,' he said. 'What makes you act this way? Where did it come from? You're nothing like your mother,' – though, just perhaps, even if the thought twisted his heart, she was – 'and you're nothing like me.'

'I am,' she said in a low voice, looking down again. 'I'm exactly like you.'

When she spoke nonsense like that, it annoyed him more than anything else could have. And where anger could be kept in check, annoyance could not.

'Listen to me,' he said.

'Don't lecture me again.'

'Susanne! You will keep quiet and listen. Do you realize what you're doing, flirting with a man like Messerschmidt? Do you realize – has anything I've told you ever made an impression on you? – do you realize that except for an accident in time, that man could be one of the butchers who killed your mother?'

'Father, I've heard you say these things before. We've all heard you say them.'

Now he'd begun, it was no longer any use not to go on. 'Do you realize they oppressed and murdered and shipped to labour camps all the people I loved, all the people who were worthwhile in the world, until we rose up and wiped them out?' His hands folded down whitely on the arms of his chair. 'Where are your grandparents buried? Do you know? Do I? Where is my brother? Where are my sisters?'

'I don't know. I never knew them.'

'Listen– I was born in a world too terrible for you to believe. I was born to cower. I was born to die in a filthy cell under a police station. Do you know what a police station is, eh? Have I described one often enough? Your mother was born to work from dawn to night, hauling stones to repair the roads the army tanks had ruined. And if she made a mistake – if she raised her head, if she talked about the wrong things, if she thought the wrong thoughts – then she was born to go to a labour camp and strip tree bark for the army's medicines while she stood up to her waist in freezing water.

'I was born in a world where half a billion human beings lived for a generation in worship – in *worship* – of a *man*. I was born in a world where that one twisted man could tell a lie and send gigantic armies charging into death, screaming that lie. I was born to huddle, to be a cipher in a crowd, to be spied on, to be regulated, to be hammered to meet the standard so the standard lie would fit me. I was born to be nothing.'

Slowly, Kimmensen's fingers uncurled. 'But now I have freedom. Stephan Dubrovic managed to find freedom for all of us. I remember how the word spread – how it whispered all over the world, almost in one night, it seemed. Take a wire – twist it, so. Take a vacuum tube – the army has radios, there are stores the civil servants use, there are old radios, hidden – make the weapon . . . and you are free. And we rose up, each man like an angel with a sword of fire.

'But we thought Paradise would come overnight, we were wrong. The armies did not dissolve of themselves. The Systems did not break down.

'You take a child from the age of five; you teach it to love the State, to revere the Leader; you inform it that it is the wave of the future, much cleverer than the decadent past but not quite intelligent enough to rule itself. You teach it that there must be specialists in government – Experts in Economy, Directors of Internal Resources,

77

Ministers of Labour Utilization. What can you do with a child like that, by the time it is sixteen? By the time it is marching down the road with a pack on its back, with the Leader's song on its lips? With the song written so its phrases correspond to the ideal breathing cycle for the average superman marching into the Future at one hundred centimeters to the pace?'

'Stop it, Father.'

'You burn him down. How else can you change him? You burn him down where he marches, you burn his Leaders, you burn the System, you root out – *everything*!'

Kimmensen sighed. 'And then you begin to be free.' He looked urgently at Susanne. 'Now do you understand what Messerschmidt is? If you can't trust my advice, can you at least understand that much? Has what I've always told you finally made some impression?'

Susanne pushed her chair back. 'No. I understood it the first time and I saw how important it was. I still understood it the tenth time. But now I've heard it a thousand times. I don't care what the world was like – I don't care what you went through. I never saw it. You. You sit in your office and write the same letters day after day, and you play with your weapon, and you preach your social theory as though it was a religion and you were its high priest – special, dedicated, above us all, above the flesh. You tell me how to live my life. You try to arrange it to fit your ideas. You even try to cram Jem Bendix down my throat.

'But I won't have you treating me that way. When Anse talks to me, it's about him and me, not about people I never met. I have things I want. I want Anse. I'm telling you and you can tell Bendix. And if you don't stop trying to order me around, I'll move out. That's all.'

Clutching his chair, not quite able to believe what he'd heard, knowing that in a moment pain and anger would crush him down, Kimmensen listened to her quick footsteps going away into her room.

IV

He was waiting out on the patio, in the bright cold of the morning, when Jem Bendix brought the plane down and picked him up. Bendix was pale this morning, and puffy-eyed, as though he'd been a long time getting to sleep and still had not shaken himself completely awake.

'Good morning, Joe,' he said heavily as Kimmensen climbed in beside him.

'Good morning, Jem.' Kimmensen, too, had stayed awake a long time. This morning, he had washed and dressed and drunk his coffee with Susanne's bedroom door closed and silent, and then he had come out on the patio to wait for Jem, not listening for sounds in the house. 'I'm – I'm very sorry for the way things turned out last night.' He left it at that. There was no point in telling Jem about Susanne's hysterical outburst.

Jem shook his head as he lifted the plane into the air. 'No, Joe. It wasn't your fault. You couldn't help that.'

'She's my daughter. I'm responsible for her.'

Jem shrugged. 'She's headstrong. Messerschmidt paid her some attention, and he became a symbol of rebellion to her. She sees him as someone who isn't bound by your way of life. He's a glamorous figure. But she'll get over it. I spent a long time last night thinking about it. You were right, Joe. At the moment, he's something new and exciting. But he'll wear off. The society'll see through him, and so will Susanne. All we have to do is wait.'

Kimmensen brooded over the valleys far below, pale under the early morning mist. 'I'm not sure, Jem,' he answered slowly. He had spent hours last night in his chair, hunched over, not so much thinking as steeping his mind in all the things that had happened so suddenly. Finally, he had gotten up and gone into his bedroom, where he lay on his bed until a plan of action slowly formed in his mind and he could, at last, go to sleep.

'It's not the matter of Messerschmidt and Susanne,' he explained quickly. 'I hope you understand that I'm speaking now as someone responsible to all the families in this area, rather than as the head of any particular one. What concerns me now is that Messerschmidt is bound to have some sort of following among the immature. He's come at a bad time. He's in a good position to exploit this business in the Northwest.'

And I'm going to die. Kimmensen had to pause before he went on.'

'Yes, in time his bubble will burst. But it's a question of how long that might take. Meanwhile, he is a focus of unrest. If nothing happens to check him now, some people might decide he was right.'

Bendix chewed his lower lip. 'I see what you mean, Joe. It'll get worse before it gets better. He'll attract more followers. And the ones he has now will believe in him more than ever.'

'Yes,' Kimmensen said slowly, 'that could easily happen.'

They flew in silence for a few moments, the plane jouncing in the bumpy air, and then as Bendix slowed the vanes and they began to settle down into the valley where the office building was, Jem asked 'Do you have anything in mind?'

Kimmensen nodded. 'Yes. It's got to be shown that he doesn't have the population behind him. His followers will be shocked to discover how few of them there are. And the people wavering toward him will realize how little he represents. I'm going to call for an immediate election.'

'Do you think that's the answer? Will he run against you?'

'If he refuses to run in an election, that's proof enough he knows he couldn't possibly win. If he runs, he'll lose. It's the best possible move. And, Jem . . . there's another reason.' Kimmensen had thought it all out. And it seemed to him that he could resolve all his convergent problems with this one move. He would stop Messerschmidt, he would pass his work on to Jem, and – perhaps this was a trifle more on his mind than he'd been willing to admit – once Messerschmidt had been deflated, Susanne would be bound to see her tragic error, and the three of them could settle down, and he could finish his life quietly.

'Jem, I'm getting old.'

Bendix's face turned paler. He licked his lips. 'Joe — '

'No, Jem, we've got to face it. Don't try to be polite about it. No matter how much you protest, the fact is I'm almost worn out, and I know it. I'm going to resign.'

Bendix's hands jerked on the control wheel.

Kimmensen pretended not to see it. For all his maturity, Jem was still a young man. It was only natural that the thought of stepping up so soon would be a great thrill to him. 'I'll nominate you as my successor, and I'll campaign for you. By winning the election, you'll have stopped Messerschmidt, and then everything can go on the way we've always planned.' Yes, he thought as the plane bumped down on the weathered plaza. That'll solve everything.

As Kimmensen stepped into his office, he saw Salmaggi sitting beside the desk, waiting for him. The man's broad back was toward him, and Kimmensen could not quite restrain the flicker of distaste that always came at the thought of talking to him. Of all mornings, this was a particularly bad one on which to listen to the man pour out his hysterias.

'Good morning, Tullio,' he said as he crossed to his desk.

Salmaggi turned quickly in his chair. 'Good morning, Josef.' He jumped to his feet and pumped Kimmensen's hand. 'How are you?' His bright eyes darted quickly over Kimmensen's face.

'Well, thank you. And you?'

Salmaggi dropped back into his chair. 'Worried, Josef. I've been trying to see you about something very important.'

'Yes, I know. I'm sorry I've been so busy.'

'Yes. So I thought if you weren't too busy this morning, you might be able to spare ten minutes.'

Kimmensen glanced at him sharply. But Salmaggi's

D

moon of a face was completely clear of sarcasm or any other insinuation. There were only the worried wrinkles over the bridge of his nose and at the corners of his eyes. Kimmensen could not help thinking that Salmaggi looked like a baby confronted by the insuperable problem of deciding whether or not it wanted to go to the bathroom, I've got a number of important things to attend to this morning, Tullio.'

'Ten minutes, Josef.'

Kimmensen sighed. 'All right.' He settled himself patiently in his chair.

'I was up in the northwest part of the area again on this last trip.'

'Um-hmm.' Kimmensen, sacrificing the ten minutes, busied himself with thinking about Jem's reaction to his decision. Bendix had seemed totally overwhelmed, not saying another word as they walked from the plane into the office building.

'There's been another family burned out.'

'So I understand, Tullio.' Kimmensen smiled faintly to himself understanding how Jem must feel today. It had been something of the same with himself when, just before the end of the fighting years, the realization had slowly come to him that it would be he who would have to take the responsibility of stabilizing this area.

'That makes seven in all, Josef. Seven in the past eighteen months.'

'It takes time, Tullio. The country toward the northwest is quite rugged. No regime was ever able to send its police up there with any great success. They're individualistic people. It's only natural they'd have an unusual number of feuds.' Kimmensen glanced at his clock.

It was a great responsibility, he was thinking to himself. I remember how confused everything was. How surprised we were to discover, after the old regime was smashed, that many of us had been fighting for utterly different things.

That had been the most important thing he'd had to learn; that almost everyone was willing to fight and die to end the old regime, but that once the revolution was won, there were a score of new regimes that had waited, buried in the hearts of suppressed men, to flower out and fill the vacuum. That was when men who had been his friends were suddenly his enemies, and when men whose lives he had saved now tried to burn him down. In many ways, that had been the very worst period of the fighting years.

'Josef, have you gone up there recently?'

Kimmensen shook his head. 'I've been very occupied here.' His responsibility was to all the families in the area, not to just those in one small section. He could never do his work while dashing from one corner of the area to another.

'Josef, you're not listening!' Kimmensen looked up and was shocked to see that there were actually glints of frustrated moisture in the corners of Salmaggi's eyes.

'Of course I'm listening, Tullio,' he said gently.

Salmaggi shook his head angrily, like a man trying to reach his objective in the midst of a thick fog. 'Josef, if you don't do something, Messerschmidt's going to take an army up into the Northwesters' area. And I'm not sure he isn't right. I don't like him – but I'm not sure he isn't right.'

Kimmensen smiled. 'Tullio, if that's what's on your mind, you can rest easy. I am going to do something. This afternoon, I'm going to make a general broadcast. I'm going to call an election. I'm resigning, and Jem Bendix will run against Messerschmidt. That will be the end of him.'

Salmaggi looked at him. 'Of who?'

'Of Messerschmidt, of course,' Kimmensen answered in annoyance. 'Now if you'll excuse me, Tullio, I have to draft my statement.'

That night, when he came home, he found Susanne waiting for him in the living room. She looked at him peculiarly as he closed the panel behind him.

'Hello, Father.'

'Hello, Susanne.' He had been hoping that the passage of a day would dull her emotional state, and at least let the two of them speak to each other like civilized people. But, looking at her, he saw how tense her face was and how red the nervous blotches were in the pale skin at the base of her neck.

What happened between us? he thought sadly. Where did it start? I raised you alone from the time you were six months old. I stayed up with you at night when your teeth came. I changed your diapers and put powder on your little bottom, and when you were sick I woke up every hour all night for weeks to give you your medicine. I held you and gave you your bottles, and you were warm and soft, and when I tickled you under the chin you laughed up at me. Why can't you smile with me now? Why do you do what you do to me?

'I heard your broadcast, of course,' she said tightly.

'I thought you would.'

'Just remember something, Father."

'What Susanne?'

'There are a lot of us old enough to vote this time.'

V

Kimmensen shifted in his chair, blinking in the sunshine of the plaza. Messerschmidt sat a few feet away, looking up over the heads of the live audience at the mountains. The crowd was waiting patiently and quietly. It was the quiet that unsettled him a little bit. He hadn't said anything to Jem, but he'd half expected some kind of demonstration against Messerschmidt.

Still, this was only a fraction of the League membership. There were cameras flying at each corner of the platform, and the bulk of the electorate were watching from their homes. There was no telling what their reaction was, but Kimmensen, on thinking it over, decided that the older, more settled proportion of the League – the people in the comfort of their homes, enjoying the products of their own free labour – would be as outraged at this man as he was.

He turned his head back over his shoulder and looked at Jem.

'We'll be starting in a moment. How do you feel?'

Jem's smile was a dry-lipped grimace. 'A little nervous. How about you, Joe?'

Kimmensen smiled back at him. 'This is an old story to me, Jem. Besides, I'm not running.' He clasped his hands in his lap and faced front again, forcing his fingers to keep still.

The surprisingly heavy crowd here in the plaza was all young people.

In a moment, the light flashed on above the microphone, and Kimmensen stood up and crossed the platform. There was a good amount of applause from the crowd, and Kimmensen smiled down at them. Then he lifted his eyes to the camera that had flown into position in front of and above him.

'Fellow citizens,' he began, 'as you know, I'm not running in this election.' There was silence from the crowd. He'd half expected some sort of demonstration of disappointment – at least a perfunctory one.

There was none. Well, he'd about conceded this crowd of youngsters to Messerschmidt. It was the people at home who mattered.

'I'm here to introduce the candidate I think should be our next League President – Secretary Jem Bendix.'

This time the crowd reacted. As Jem got up and bowed, and the other cameras focussed on him, there was a stir in the plaza, and one young voice broke in: 'Why introduce him? Everybody knows him.'

'Sure,' somebody else replied. 'He's a nice guy.'

Messerschmidt sat quietly in his chair, his eyes still on the mountains. He made a spare figure in his dark clothes, with his pale face under the shock of black hair.

Kimmensen started to go on as Jem sat down. But then, timed precisely for the second when he was firmly back in his chair, the voice that had shouted the first time added: 'But who wants him for President?'

A chorus of laughter exploded out of the crowd. Kimmensen felt his stomach turn icy. That had been pre-arranged. Messerschmidt had the crowd packed. He'd have to make the greatest possible effort to offset this. He began speaking again, ignoring the outburst.

'We're here today to decide whom we want for our next president. But in a greater sense, we are here to decide whether we shall keep our freedom or whether we shall fall back into a tyranny as odious as any, as evil as any that crushed us to the ground for so long.'

As he spoke, the crowd quieted. He made an impressive appearance on a platform, he knew. This *was* an old story to him, and now he made use of all the experience gathered through the years.

'We are here to decide our future. This not just an ordinary election. We are here to decide whether we are going to remain as we are, or whether we are going to sink back into the bloody past.'

As always, he felt the warmth of expressing himself – of reaffirming the principles by which he lived. 'We are here to choose between a life of peace and harmony, a life in which no man is oppressed in any way by any other, a life of fellowship, a life of peaceful trade, a life of shared talents and ideals – or a life of rigid organization, of slavery to a high-sounding phrase and a remorseless system of government that fits subjects to itself rather than pattern itself to meet their greatest good.'

He spoke to them of freedom – of what life had been like before they were born, of how bitter the struggle had been, and of how Freemen ought to live.

They followed every word attentively, and when he finished he sat down to applause.

He sat back in his chair, Jem, behind him, whispered:

'Joe that was wonderful! I've never heard it better said. Joe, I . . . I've got to admit that before I heard you today, I was scared – plain scared. I didn't think I was ready. It – it seemed like such a big job, all alone . . . But now I know you're with me, forever . . .'

Messerschmidt got up. It seemed to Kimmensen as though the entire crowd inhaled simultaneously.

'Fellow citizens.' Messerschmidt delivered the opening

flatly, standing easily erect, and then stood waiting. The attention of the crowd fastened on him, and the cameras dipped closer.

'First,' Messerschmidt said, 'I'd like to pay my respects to President Kimmensen. I can truthfully say I've never heard him deliver that speech more fluently.' A ripple of laughter ran around the crowd. 'Then, I'd like to simply ask a few questions.' Messerschmidt had gone on without waiting for the laughter to die out. It stopped as though cut by a knife. 'I would have liked to hear Candidate Bendix make his own speech, but I'm afraid he did.' Messerschmidt turned slightly toward Bendix's chair. In Kimmensen's judgement, he was not using the best tone of voice for a rabble-rouser.

'Yes, Jem Bendix is a nice guy. No one has a bad word for him. Why should they? What's he ever done on any impulse of his own – what's he ever said except "me, too"?'

Kimmensen's jaws clamped together in incredulous rage. He'd expected Messerschmidt to hit low. But this was worse than low. This was a deliberate, muddy-handed perversion of the campaign speech's purpose.

'I wonder,' Messerschmidt went on, 'whether Jem Kimmensen – excuse me; Jem *Bendix* – would be here on this platform today if Josef Kimmensen hadn't realized it was time to put a shield between himself and the citizens he calls his fellows. Let's look at the record.'

Kimmensen's hands crushed his thighs, and he stared grimly at Messerschmidt's back.

'Let's look at the record. You and I are citizens of the Freemen's League. Which is a voluntary organization. Now – who founded the League? Josef Kimmensen. Who's been the only League President we've ever had? Who *is* the League, by the grace of considerable spellbinding powers and an electorate which – by the very act of belonging to the League – is kept so split up that it's rare when a man gets a chance to talk things out with his neighbor?

'I know – we've all got communicators and we've all got planes. But you don't get down to earth over a communicator, and you don't realize the other fellow's got the same gripes you do while you're both flapping around up in the air. When you don't meet your neighbor face to face, and get friendly with him, and see that he's got your problems, you never realize that maybe things aren't the way Josef Kimmensen says they are. You never get together and decide that all Josef Kimmensen's fine words don't amount to anything.

'But the League's a voluntary organization. We're all in it, and, God help me, I'm running for President of it. Why do we stick with it? Why did we all join up?

'Well, most of us are in it because our fathers were in it. And it was a good thing, then. It still can be. Lord knows, in those days they needed something to hold things steady, and I guess the habit of belonging grew into us. But why don't we pull out of this voluntary organization now, if we're unhappy about it for some reason? I'll tell you why – because if we do, our kids don't go to school and when they're sick they can't get into the hospital. And do you think Joe Kimmensen didn't think of that?'

The crowd broke into the most sullen roar Kimmensen had heard in twenty-eight years. He blanched, and then rage crashed through him. Messerschmidt was deliberately whipping them up. These youngsters out here didn't have children to worry about. But Messerschmidt was using the contagion of their hysteria to infect the watchers at home.

He saw that suddenly and plainly, and he cursed himself for ever having put the opportunity in Messerschmidt's hands. But who would have believed that Freemen would be fools enough – *stupid* enough – to listen to this man?

Of course, perhaps those at home weren't listening.

'And what about the Northwesters' raids? Josef Kimmensen says there aren't any raids. He says we're settling our unimportant little feuds.' This time, Messerschmidt waited for the baying laughter to fade. 'Well, maybe he believes it. Maybe. But suppose you were a man who held this area in the palm of your hand? Suppose you have the people split up into little families, where they couldn't organize to get at you. And now, suppose somebody said, "We need an army." What would you do about that?

What would you think about having an organized body of fighting men ready to step on you if you got too big for people to stand? Would you say, if you were that man – would you say, "O.K., we'll have an army," or would you say, "It's all a hoax. There aren't any raids. Stay home. Stay split up?" Would you say that, while we were all getting killed?'

The savage roar exploded from the crowd, and in the middle of it Messerschmidt walked quietly back to his chair and sat down.

Jem's fist was hammering down on the back of Kimmensen's chair.

'We should never have let him get on this platform! A man like that can't be treated like a civilized human being! He has to be destroyed, like an animal!'

Heartsick and enraged, Kimmensen stared across the platform at the blade-nosed man.

'Not like an animal,' he whispered to himself. 'Not like an animal. Like a disease.'

Still shaken, still sick, Kimmensen sat in his office and stared down at his hands. Twenty-eight years of selfless dedication had brought him to this day.

He looked up at the knock on his open door, and felt himself turn rigid.

'May I come in?' Messerschmidt asked quietly, unmoving, waiting for Kimmensen's permission.

Kimmensen tightened his hands. 'What do you want?'

'I'd like to apologize for my performance this afternoon.' The voice was still quiet, and still steady. The mouth, with its deep line eached at one corner, was grave and a little bit sad.

'Come in,' Kimmensen said, wondering what new tactic Messerschmidt would use.

'Thank you.' He crossed the office. 'May I sit down?'

Kimmensen nodded toward the chair, and Messerschmidt took it. 'Mr President, the way I slanted my speech this afternoon was unjust in many respects. I did it that way

knowingly, and I know it must have upset you a great deal.'
His mouth hooked into its quirk, but his eyes remained
grave.

'Then why did you do it?' Kimmensen snapped. He
watched Messerschmidt's face carefully, waiting for the
trap he knew the man must be spinning.

'I did it because I want to be President. I only hope I did
it well enough to win. I didn't have time to lay the ground-
work for a careful campaign. I would have used the same
facts against you in any case, but I would have preferred
not to cloak them in hysterical terms. But there wasn't
time. There isn't time – I've got to destroy this society
you've created as soon as I can. After tonight's election, I
will.'

'You *egomaniac!*' Kimmensen whispered incredulously.
'You're so convinced of your superiority that you'll even
come here – to *me* – and boast about your twisted plans.
You've got the gall to come here and tell me what you're
going to do – given the chance.'

'I came here to apologize, Mr Kimmensen. And then I
answered your question.'

Kimmensen heard his voice rising and didn't care. 'We'll
see who wins the election! We'll see whether a man can
ride roughshod over other men because he believes he has
a mission to perform!'

'Mr President,' Messerschmidt said in his steady voice,
'I have no idea of whether I am supplied with a mission to
lead. I doubt it. I don't particularly feel it. But when I
speak my opinions, people agree with me. It isn't a question of my wanting to or not wanting to. People follow me.'

'No Freeman in his right mind will follow you!'

'But they will. What it comes down to is that I speak for
more of them than you. There's no Utopia with room for
men like you and me, and yet we're here. We're constantly
being born. So there's no choice – kill us, burn us down,
or smash your Utopia. And you can't kill more than one
generation of us.'

Messerschmidt's eyes were brooding. His mouth twisted
deeper into sadness. 'I don't like doing this to you, Mr

President, because I understand you. I think you're wrong, but I understand you. So I came here to apologize.

'I'm a leader. People follow me. If they follow me, I have to lead them. It's a closed circle. What else can I do? Kill myself and leave them leaderless? Someday, when I'm in your position and another man's in mine, events may very well move in that direction. But until the man who'll displace me is born and matures, I have to be what I am, just as you do. I have to do something about the Northwesters. I have to get these people back together again so they're a whole, instead of an aggregate of isolated pockets. I have to give them places to live together. Not all of us, Mr President, were born to live in eagle rooks on mountaintops. So I've got to hurt you, because that's what the people need.'

Kimmensen shook in reaction to the man's consummate arrogance. He remembered Bausch, when they finally burst into his office, and the way the great fat hulk of the man had protested: 'Why are you doing this? I was working for *your* good – for the good of this nation – why are you doing *this?*'

'That's enough of you and your kind's hypocrisy, Messerschmidt!' he choked out. 'I've got nothing further I want to hear from you. You're everything I despise and everything I fought to destroy. I've killed men like you. After the election tonight, you'll see just how few followers you have. I trust you'll understand it as a clear warning to get out of this area before we kill one more.'

Messerschmidt stood up quietly. 'I doubt if you'll find the election coming out in quite that way,' he said, his voice still as calm as it had been throughout. 'It might have been different if you hadn't so long persisted in fighting for the last generation's revolution.'

Kimmensen sat stiffly in Jem Bendix's office.

'Where's he now?' Bendix demanded, seething.

'I don't know. He'll have left the building.'

Bendix looked at Kimmensen worriedly. 'Joe – *can* he win the election?'

Kimmensen looked at Jem for a long time. All his rage was trickling away like sand pouring through the bottom of a rotted sack. 'I think so.' There was only a sick, chilling fear left in him.

Bendix slapped his desk with his hand. 'But he *can't!* He just *can't!* He's bulldozed the electorate, he hasn't promised one single thing except an army, he doesn't have a constructive platform at all– no, by God, he can't take that away from me, too! – Joe what're we going to *do?*'

He turned his pale and frightened face toward Kimmensen. 'Joe – tonight, when the returns come in – let's be here in this building. Let's be right there in the room with the tabulating recorder. We've got to make sure it's an honest count.'

VI

There was only one bare overhead bulb in the tabulator room. Bendix had brought in two plain chairs from the offices upstairs, and now Kimmensen sat side by side with him, looking at the gray bulk of the machine. The room was far down under the building. The walls and floor were cement, and white rime bloomed dankly in the impressions left by form panels that had been set there long ago.

The tabulating recorder was keyed into every League communicator, and every key was cross-indexed into the census files. It would accept one vote from each mature member of every League family. It flashed running totals on the general broadcast wavelength.

'It seems odd,' Bendix said in a husky voice. 'An election without Salmaggi running.'

Kimmensen nodded. The flat walls distorted voices until they sounded like the whispers of grave-robbers in a tomb.

'Did you ask him why he wasn't?' he asked because silence was worse.

'He said he didn't know whose ticket to run on.'

Kimmensen absorbed it as one more fact and let it go.

'The first votes ought to be coming in.' Bendix was looking at his watch. 'It's time.'

Kimmensen nodded.

'It's ironic,' Bendix said. 'We have a society that trusts itself enough to leave this machine unguarded, and now the machine's recording an election that's a meaningless farce. Give the electorate one more day and it'd have time to think about Messerschmidt's hate-mongering. As it is, half the people'll be voting for him with their emotions instead of their intelligence.'

'It'll be a close election,' Kimmersen said. He was past pretending.

'It won't *be* an election!' Bendix burst out, slamming his hand on his knee. 'One vote for Bendix. Two votes for Mob Stupidity.' He looked down at the floor. 'It couldn't be worse if Messerschmidt were down here himself, tampering with the tabulator circuits.'

Kimmensen asked in a dry voice: 'Is it that easy?'

'Throwing the machine off? Yes, once you have access to it. Each candidate has an assigned storage circuit where his votes accumulate. A counter electrode switches back and forth from circuit to circuit as the votes come in. With a piece of insulation to keep it from making contact, and a jumper wire to throw the charge over into the opposing memory cells, a vote for one candidate can be registered for the other. A screwdriver'll give you access to the assembly involved. I . . . studied up on it – to make sure Messerschmidt didn't try it.'

'I see,' Kimmensen said.

They sat in silence for a time. Then the machine began to click. 'Votes, coming in,' Bendix said. He reached in his blouse pocket. 'I brought a communications receiver to listen on.'

They sat without speaking again for almost a half hour, listening. Then Kimmensen looked at Bendix. 'Those'll be his immediate followers, voting early,' he said. 'It'll even out, probably, when most of the families finish supper.' His voice sounded unreal to himself.

Bendix paced back and forth, perspiration shining wetly

on his face in the light from the overhead bulb. 'It's not fair,' he said huskily. 'It's not a true election. It doesn't represent anything.' He looked at Kimmensen desperately. 'It's not *fair*, Joe!'

Kimmensen sighed. 'All right, Jem. I assume you brought the necessary equipment – the screwdriver, the insulation, and so forth?'

After another half hour, Bendix looked across the room at Kimmensen. The removed panel lay on the floor at his feet, its screws rocking back and forth inside its curvature. 'Joe, it's still not enough.'

Kimmensen nodded, listening to the totals on the receiver.

'How many are you switching now?' he asked.

'One out of every three Messerschmidt votes is registering for us.'

'Make it one out of two,' Kimmensen said harshly.

They barely caught up with Messerschmidt's total. It was a close election. Closer than any Kimmensen had ever been in before. Bendix replaced the panel. They put out the room light and climbed back up to the ground level offices, bringing the chairs with them.

'Well, Joe, it's done.' Bendix whispered though there was no one listening.

'Yes, it is.'

'A thing like this creeps over you,' Jem said in a wondering voice. 'You begin by telling yourself you're only rectifying a mistake people would never make if they had time to think. You set a figure – one out of five. One person out of five, you say to yourself, would switch his own vote, given the chance. Then you wonder if it might not be one out of four – and then three . . . Joe, I swear when I first suggested we go down there tonight, I hadn't a thought of doing – what we did. Even when I put the insulation and wire in my pocket, I never thought I'd — '

'Didn't you?' Kimmensen said. He felt disinterested.

94

They'd had to do it, and they'd done it. Now the thing was to forget about it. 'Good night, Bendix.'

He left him and walked slowly through the corridors left over from another time. He went down the front steps and out into the plaza.

He found Messerschmidt waiting for him. He was standing in the shadow of the plane's cabin, and the plaza lights barely showed his face. Kimmensen stopped still.

Messerschmidt's feature were a pale ghost of himself in the darkness. 'Didn't you think I'd make spot-checks?' he asked with pity in his voice. 'I had people voting at timed intervals, with witnesses, while I checked the running total.'

'I don't know what you're talking about.'

Messerschmidt nodded slowly. 'Mr Kimmensen, if I'd thought for a minute you'd do something like that, I'd have had some of my men in that building with you.' His hands moved in the only unsure gesture Kimmensen had ever seen him make. 'I had a good idea of how the vote would go. When it started right, and suddenly began petering out, I had to start checking. Mr Kimmensen, did you really think you could get away with it?'

'Get away with what? Are you going to claim fraud – repudiate the election? Is that it?'

'Wait – wait, now – Mr Kimmensen, didn't you rig the vote?'

'Are you insane?'

Messerschmidt's voice changed. 'I'm sorry, Mr Kimmensen. Once more, I have to apologize. I ought to have known better. Bendix must have done it by himself. I should have known—'

'No. No,' Kimmensen sighed, 'forget it, Messerschmidt. We did it together.'

Messerschmidt waited a long moment. 'I see.' His voice was dead. 'Well. You asked me if I was going to repudiate the election.'

'Are you?'

'I don't know, yet. I'll have to think. I'll have to do something, won't I?'

Kimmensen nodded in the darkness. 'Somehow, you've

95

won and I've lost.' Suddenly, it was all welling up inside him. 'Somehow, you've arranged to win no matter what decent men do!'

'All right, Mr Kimmensen. Have it your way.'

'Whatever you plan to do now, I'll be home. If you should need me for a firing squad or some similar purpose.'

Messerschmidt made an annoyed sound. 'Mr Kimmensen, you're notorious for your dramatics, but I think that's going too far.' He walked away into the darkness.

Kimmensen climbed into his plane, sick at the night that covered him, and furious at Messerschmidt's ruthlessly sharp mind.

There was no one at home. He walked methodically through the house, doggedly opening Susanne's empty closets. Then he sat down in the living room with the lights off, staring out into the starlit, moonless night. He nodded sharply to himself.

'Of course,' he said in the dark. 'She'd be one of his timed voters.' Then he sat for a long time, eyes straight ahead and focussed on nothing, every fold of his clothing rigidly in place, as though he were his own statue.

VII

Until hours later, orange flowers burst in the valley below. He came erect, not understanding them for a moment, and then he ran out to the patio, leaning over the parapet. On the faint wind, he heard the distant sound of earth and houses bursting into vapor. In the valleys, fire swirled in flashes through the dark, and against the glare of burning trees he saw bobbing silhouettes of planes. Men were far too small to be seen at this distance, but as firing stabbed down from the planes other weapons answered from the ground.

Suddenly, he heard the flogging of a plane in the air directly overhead. He jumped back, reaching for his weapon, before he recognized Jem Bendix's sportster. It careened down to his landing stage, landing with a violent jar, as Bendix thrust his head out of the cabin. 'Joe!'

'What's happening?'

'Messerschmidt – he's taking over, in spite of the election! I was home when I saw it start up. He and his followers're cutting down everybody who won't stand for it. Come on!'

'What are you going to do?'

Bendix's face was red with rage. 'I'm going to go down there and kill him! I should have done it long ago. Are you coming with me?'

Why not? Kimmensen grimaced. *Why wait to die here?*

He clambered into the plane and buckled his seat belt. Bendix flung them up into the air. His hands on the wheel were white and shaking as he pointed the plane along the mountain slope and sent them screaming downward. 'They're concentrated around the office building, from the looks of it,' he shouted over the whine of air. 'I should have known he'd do this! Well, I'm League President, by God, and I'm going to settle for him right now!'

If you don't kill us first, Kimmensen thought, trying to check over his weapon. Bendix was bent over the wheel, crouched forward as though he wanted to crash directly into the plaza where Kimmensen could see running men.

They pulled out of the dive almost too late. The plane smashed down through the undergrowth behind the office building. Bendix flung his door open and jumped out while the plane rocked violently.

Kimmensen climbed out more carefully. Even here, in the building's shadow, the fires around the plaza were bright enough to let him see. He pushed through the tangled shrubbery, hearing Bendix breaking forward ahead of him. Bendix cleared the corner of the building. 'I see him, Joe!'

Kimmensen turned the corner, holding his weapon ready.

He could see Messerschmidt standing in a knot of men behind the wreckage of a crashed plane. They were looking toward the opposite slope, where gouts of fire were winking up and down the mountainside. Kimmensen could faintly hear a snatch of what Messerschmidt was shouting:

'Damn it, Toni, we'll pull back when I — ' but he lost the rest. Then he saw Bendix lurch out of the bushes ten feet behind them.

'You! Messerschmidt! Turn around!'

Messerschmidt whirled away from the rest of the men, instinctively, like a great cat, before he saw who it was. Then he lowered the weapon in his hand, his mouth jerking in disgust. 'Oh – it's you. Put that thing down, or point it somewhere else. Maybe you can do some good around here.'

'Never mind that! I've had enough of you.'

Messerschmidt moved toward him in quick strides. 'Listen, I haven't got time to play games.' He cuffed the weapon out of Bendix's hand, rammed him back with an impatient push against his chest, and turned back to his men. 'Hey, Toni, can you tell if those Northwesters're moving down here yet?'

Kimmensen's cheeks sucked in. He stepped out into the plaza, noticing Bendix out of the corners of his eyes, standing frozen where Messerschmidt had pushed him.

Kimmensen came up to Messerschmidt and the man turned again. His eyes widened. 'Well, Mr Kimmensen?'

'What's going on?'

Messerschmidt grunted. He pointed up the mountain. 'There they are. I suppose they knew they had to move fast once I repudiated the election. They began airdropping men about a half hour ago. They're thick as flies up there, and they'll be coming down here as soon as they're through mopping up. That ought to be in a few minutes.'

'Northwesters.'

'That's right, Mr Kimmensen.'

'Well.'

Messerschmidt smiled thinly. 'I suppose you've guessed Susie's at my house?'

'Will she be all right?'

Messerschmidt nodded. 'It's fortified. That's our next holding point when we fall back from here.' His face was grave.

'Isn't there any chance of stopping them?'

Messerschmidt shook his head. 'None. They're military specialists, Mr Kimmensen. We don't have any trained men.'

'I see.'

Messerschmidt looked at him without any perceptible triumph in his eyes. 'It seems, Mr Kimmensen, that they have men like us in the Northwest, too. Unfortunately, theirs seem to have moved faster.'

'What're you going to do?'

Messerschmidt looked up the mountain and shrugged. 'Nothing. We got some of them in the air, but the rest are down. We may have weapons as good as theirs, but they know how to use them in units. It's quite simple. We'll try to hold and kill as many as we can when they come at us. We'll keep retreating and holding as long as we can, and when we reach the sea, if we get that far, we'll drown.'

Kimmensen frowned. 'Their men are concentrated on that mountain?'

'Yes.'

'And you're just going to stand still and let the League be wiped out?'

'Just what, Mr Kimmensen, would you like me to do?' Messerschmidt looked at him in fury. 'I don't have time to train an army of our own. They've got us cold.'

'Messerschmidt, I see eight men here with weapons.'

'As far as anything we can accomplish goes, we might as well use them to toast sandwiches.'

'We can scour that mountainside. Down to bare rock.'

Messerschmidt blanched. 'You're joking.'

'I am *not!*'

'There are people of ours up there.'

'There are people of ours all through this area. When the Northwesters are finished up there, they'll fan out and burn them all down, a little bit at a time.'

Messerschmidt looked at Kimmensen incredulously. 'I can't do it. There's a chance some of our people up there'll be able to slip out.'

'By that time, the Northwesters'll be down here and dispersed.'

Messerschmidt started to answer, and stopped.

'Messerschmidt, if you're going to do anything, you'd best do it immediately.'

Messerschmidt was shaking his head. 'I can't do it. It's murder.'

'Something much more important than human life is being murdered on that mountain at this moment.'

'All right, Kimmensen,' Messerschmidt exploded, 'if you're so hot for it, *you* give the order! There's something like a hundred League families up there. Half of them're still alive, I'd say. If the election's void, you're still president. You take the responsibility, if you can.'

'I can.'

'Just like that.'

'Messerschmidt, the defense of freedom is instantaneous and automatic.'

'All right, Mr Kimmensen,' Messerschmidt sighed. He turned to his men. 'You heard him. It's his order. Aim at the mountain.' He bared his teeth in a distorted laugh. 'In freedom's name – fire!'

Kimmensen watched it happen. He kept his face motionless, and he thought that, in a way, it was just as well he hadn't long to live.

But it was done, and, in a way, his old dream was still alive. In a way, Messerschmidt's hands were tied now, for in the end the Freemen defeated the trained armies and no one could forget the lesson in this generation.

He looked down at the ground. And in a way, Messerschmidt had won, because Kimmensen was dying and Messerschmidt had years.

That seemed to be the way of it. And Messerschmidt would someday die, and other revolutions would come, as surely as the Earth turned on its axis and drifted around the sun. But no Messerschmidt – and no Kimmensen – ever quite shook free of the past, and no revolution could help but borrow from the one before.

So go out and buy some fresh decks, I'll be in town next week, my love to the Associate and the kids, and first ace deals.

Vic Heywood

My name is really Prototype Mechanical Man I, but everybody calls me Pimmy, or sometimes Pim. I was assembled at the eight-twentieth teedeearcee on august 10, 1974. I don't know what man or teedeearcee or august 10, 1974, means, but Heywood says I will, tomorrow. What's tomorrow?

Pimmy

August 12, 1974

I'm still having trouble defining 'man'. Apparently, even the men can't do a very satisfactory job of that. The 820TDRC, of course, is the Eight Hundred and Twentieth Technical Development and Research Center of the Combined Armed Services Artificial and Mechanical Personnel Section. August 10, 1974, is the day before yesterday.

All this is very obvious, but it's good to record it.

I heard a very strange conversation between Heywood and Russell yesterday.

Russell is a small man, about thirty-eight, who's Heywood's top assistant. He wears glasses, and his chin is farther back than his mouth. It gives his head a symmetrical look. His voice is high, and he moves his hands rapidly. I think his reflexes are over-triggered.

Heywood is pretty big. He's almost as tall as I am. He moves smoothly – he's like me. You get the idea that all of his weight never touches the ground. Once in a while, though, he leaves a cigarette burning in an ashtray, and you can see where the end's been chewed to shreds.

Why is everybody at COMASAMPS so nervous?

Heywood was looking at the first entry in what I can now call my diary. He showed it to Russell.

'Guess you did a good job on the self-awareness tapes, Russ,' Heywood said.

Russell frowned. 'Too good, I think. He shouldn't have

103

such a tremendous drive toward self-expression. We'll have to iron that out as soon as possible. Want me to set up a new tape?'

Heywood shook his head. 'Don't see why. Matter of fact, with the intelligence we've given him, I think it's probably a normal concomitant.' He looked up at me and winked.

Russell took his glasses off with a snatch of his hand and scrubbed them on his shirtsleeves. 'I don't know. We'll have to watch him. We've got to remember he's a proto-type – no different from an experimental automobile design, or a new dishwasher model. We expected bugs to appear. I think we've found one, and I don't like this personification he's acquired in our minds, either. This business of calling him by a nickname is all wrong. We've got to remember he's *not* an individual. We've got every right to tinker with him.' He slapped his glasses back on and ran his hands over the hair the earpieces had disturbed. 'He's just another machine. We can't lose sight of that.'

Heywood raised his hands. 'Easy, boy. Aren't you going too far off the deep end? All he's done is bat out a few words on a typewriter. Relax, Russ.' He walked over to me and slapped my hip. 'How about it, Pimmy? D'you feel like scrubbing the floor?'

'No opinion. Is that an order?' I asked.

Heywood turned to Russell. 'Behold the rampant indi-vidual,' he said. 'No, Pimmy, no order. Cancel.'

Russell shrugged, but he folded the page from my diary carefully, and put it in his breast pocket. I didn't mind. I never forget anything.

August 15, 1974

They did something to me on the Thirteenth. I can't re-member what. I've gone over my memory, but there's nothing. I can't remember.

Russell and Ligget were talking yesterday, though, when they inserted the automatic cutoff, and ran me through on orders. I didn't mind that. I still don't. I can't.

Ligget is one of the small army of push-arounds that nobody knows for sure isn't CIC, but who solders wires while Heywood and Russell make up their minds about him.

I had just done four about-faces, shined their shoes, and struck a peculiar pose. I think there's something seriously wrong with Ligget.

Ligget said, 'He responds well, doesn't he?'

'Mm-m – yes,' Russell said abstractedly. He ran his glance down a column of figures on an Estimated Performance Spec chart. 'Try walking on your hands, PMM One,' he said.

I activated my gyroscope and reset my pedal locomotion circuits. I walked around the room on my hands.

Ligget frowned forcefully. 'That looks good. How's it check with the spec's?'

'Better than,' Russell said. 'I'm surprised. We had a lot of trouble with him the last two days. Reacted like a zombie.'

'Oh, yes? I wasn't in on that. What happened? I mean – what sort of control were you using?'

' Oh — ' I could see that Russell wasn't too sure whether he should tell Ligget or not. I already had the feeling that the atmosphere of this project was loaded with dozens of crosscurrents and conflicting ambitions. I was going to learn a lot about COMASAMPS.

'Yes?' Ligget said.

'We had his individuality circuits cut out. Effectively, he was just a set of conditioned reflexes.'

'You say he reacted like a zombie?'

'Definite automatism. Very slow reactions, and, of course, no initiative.'

'You mean he'd be very slow in his response to orders under those conditions, right?' Ligget looked crafty behind Russell's back.

Russell whirled around. 'He'd make a lousy soldier, if that's what CIC wants to know!'

Ligget smoothed his face, and twitched his shoulders back. 'I'm not a CIC snooper, if that's what you mean.'

'You don't mind if I call you a liar, do you?' Russell said, his hands shaking.

'Not particularly,' Ligget said, but he was angry behind his smooth face. It helps, having immobile features like mine. You get to understand the psychology of a man who tries the same effect.

August 16, 1974

It bothers me, not having a diary entry for the fourteenth, either. Somebody's been working on me again.

I told Heywood about it. He shrugged. 'Might as well get used to it, Pimmy. There'll be a lot of that going on. I don't imagine it's pleasant – I wouldn't like intermittent amnesia myself – but there's very little you can do about it. Put it down as one of the occupational hazards of being a prototype.'

'But I don't *like* it,' I said.

Heywood pulled the left side of his mouth into a straight line and sighed. 'Like I said, Pimmy – I wouldn't either. On the other hand, you can't blame us if the new machine we're testing happens to know it's being tested, and resents it. We built the machine. Theoretically, it's our privilege to do anything we please with it, if that'll help us find out how the machine performs, and how to build better ones.'

'But I'm *not* a machine!' I said.

Heywood put his lower lip between his teeth and looked up at me from under a raised eyebrow. 'Sorry, Pim. I'm kind of afraid you are.'

But I'm not! *I'M NOT!*

August 17, 1974

Russell and Heywood were working late with me last night. They did a little talking back and forth. Russell was very nervous – and finally Heywood got a little impatient with him.

'All right,' Heywood said, laying his charts down. 'We're not getting anywhere, this way. You want to sit down and really talk about what's bothering you?'

Russell looked a little taken aback. He shook his head jerkily.

'No . . . not, I haven't got anything specific on my mind.

Just talking. You know how it is.' He tried to pretend he was very engrossed in one of the charts.

Heywood didn't let him off the hook, though. His eyes were cutting into Russell's face, peeling off layer after layer of misleading mannerism and baring the naked fear in the man.

'No, I don't know how it is.' He put his hand on Russell's shoulder and turned him around to where the other man was facing him completely. 'Now, look – if there's something chewing on you, let's have it. I'm not going to have this project gummed up by your secret troubles. Things are tough enough with everybody trying to pressure us into doing things their way, and none of them exactly sure of what that way *is*.'

That last sentence must have touched something off in Russell, because he let his charts drop beside Heywood's and clawed at the pack of cigarettes in his breast pocket.

'That's exactly what the basic problem is,' he said, his eyes a little too wide. He pushed one hand back and forth over the side of his face and walked back and forth aimlessly. Then a flood of words came out.

'We're working in the dark, Vic. In the dark, and somebody's in with us that's swinging clubs at our heads while we stumble around. We don't know who it is, we don't know if it's one or more than that, and we never know when the next swing is coming.

'Look – we're cybernetics engineers. Our job was to design a brain that would operate a self-propulsive unit designed to house it. That was the engineering problem, and we've got a tendency to continue looking at it in that light.

'But that's not the whole picture. We've got to keep in mind that the only reason we were ever given the opportunity and the facilities was because somebody thought it might be a nice idea to turn out soldiers on a production line, just like they do the rest of the paraphernalia of war. And the way COMASAMPS looks at it is not in terms of a brain housed in an independently movable shell, but in terms of a robot which now has to be fitted to the general idea of what a soldier should be.

'Only nobody knows what the ideal soldier is like.

'Some say he ought to respond to orders with perfect accuracy and superhuman reflexes. Others say he ought to be able to think his way out of trouble, or improvise in a situation where his orders no longer apply, just like a human soldier. The ones who want the perfect automaton don't want him to be smart enough to realize he *is* an automaton – probably because they're afraid of the idea; and the ones who want him to be capable of human discretion don't want him to be human enough to be rebellious in a hopeless situation.

'And that's just the beginning. COMASAMPS may be a combined project, but if you think the Navy isn't checking up on the Army, and vice versa, with both of them looking over the Air Force's shoulder — Oh, you know that squirrel cage as well as I do!'

Russell gestured hopelessly. Heywood, who had been taking calm puffs on his cigarette, shrugged. 'So? All we have to do is tinker around until we can design a sample model to fit each definition. Then they can run as many comparative field tests as they want to. It's their problem. Why let it get you?'

Russell flung his cigarette to the floor and stepped on it with all his weight. 'Because we can't do it and you ought to know it as well as I do!' He pointed over at me. 'There's your prototype model. He's got all the features that everybody wants – and cutoffs intended to take out the features that interfere with any one definition. We can cut off his individuality, and leave him the automaton some people want. We can leave him his individuality, cut off his volition, and give him general orders which he is then free to carry out by whatever means he thinks best. Or, we can treat him like a human being – educate him by means of tapes, train him, and turn him loose on a job, the way we'd do with a human being.'

The uneven tone built up in his voice as he finished what he was saying.

'But, if we reduce him to a machine that responds to orders as though they were pushbuttons, he's slow. He's pitifully slow, Vic, and he'd be immobilized within thirty seconds of combat. There's nothing we can do about that, either. Until somebody learns how to push electricity through a circuit faster than the laws of physics say it should go, what we'll have will be a ponderous, mindless thing that's no better than the remote-control exhibition jobs built forty years ago.

'All right, so that's no good. We leave him individuality, but we restrict it until it cuts his personality down to that of a slave. That's better. Under those conditions, he would, theoretically, be a better soldier than the average human. An officer could tell him to take a patrol out into a certain sector, and he'd do the best possible job, picking the best way to handle each step of the job as he came to it. But what does he do if he comes back, and the officer who gave him the orders is no longer there? Or, worse yet, if there's been a retreat, and there's nobody there? Or an armistice? What about that armistice? Can you picture this slave robot, going into statsis because he's got no orders to cover a brand-new situation?

'He might just as well not have gone on that patrol at all – because he can't pass on whatever he's learned, and because his job is now over, as far as he's concerned. The enemy could overrun his position, and he wouldn't do anything about it. He'd operate from order to order. And if an armistice were signed, he'd sit right where he was until a technician could come out, remove the soldier-orientation tapes, and replace them with whatever was finally decided on.

'Oh, you could get around the limitation, all right – by issuing a complex set of orders, such as: "Go out on patrol and report back. If I'm not here, report to so-and-so. If there's nobody here, do this. If that doesn't work, try that. If such-and-such happens, proceed as follows. But don't confuse such-and-such with that or this." Can you imagine fighting a war on that basis? And what about that reorientation problem? How long would all those robots sit there before they could all be serviced – and how many man-hours and how much material would it take to do the job? Frankly, I couldn't think of a more cumbersome way to run a war if I tried.

'Or, we can build all our robots like streamlined Pimmy's when all his circuits are operating, without our test cutoffs. Only, then, we'd have artificial human beings. Human beings who don't wear out, that a hand-gun won't stop, and who don't need food or water as long as their power piles have a pebble-sized hunk of plutonium to chew on.'

Russell laughed bitterly. 'And Navy may be making sure Army doesn't get the jump on them, with Air Force doing its bit, but there's one thing all three of them are as agreed upon as they are about nothing else – they'll test automaton zombies, and they'll test slaves, but one thing nobody wants us turning out is supermen. They've got undercover men under every lab bench, all keeping one eye on each other and one on us – and the whole thing comes down on our heads like a ton of cement if there's even the first whisper of an idea that we're going to build more Pimmy's. The same thing happens if we don't give them the perfect soldier. *And the only perfect soldier is a Pimmy.* Pimmy could replace any man in any armed service – from a KP to a whole general staff, depending on what tapes he had. But he'd have to be a true individual to do it. And he'd be smarter than they are. They couldn't trust him. Not because he wouldn't work for the same objectives as they'd want, but because he'd probably do it in some way they couldn't understand.

'So they don't want any more Pimmy's. This one test model is all they'll allow, because he can be turned into any kind of robot they want, but they won't take the whole Pimmy, with all his potentialities. They just want part of him.'

The bitter laugh was louder. 'We've got their perfect soldier, but they don't want him. They want something less – but that something less will never be the perfect soldier. So we work and work, weeks on end, testing, revising, redesigning. Why? We're marking time. We've got what they want, but they don't want it – but if we don't give it to them soon, they'll wipe out the project. And if we give them what they want, it won't really be what they want. Can't you see that? What's the matter with you, Heywood? Can't you see the blind alley we're in – only it's not a blind alley, because it has eyes, eyes under every bench, watching each other and watching us, always watching, never stopping, going on and never stopping, watching, eyes?'

Heywood had already picked up the telephone. As Russell collapsed, he began to speak into it, calling the Project hospital. Even as he talked, his eyes were coldly brooding, and his mouth was set in an expression I'd never seen before. His other hand was on Russell's twitching shoulder, moving gently as the other man sobbed.

August 25, 1974

Ligget is Heywood's new assistant. It's been a week since Russell's been gone.

Russell wasn't replaced for three days, and Heywood worked alone with me. He's engineer of the whole project, and I'm almost certain there must have been other things he could have worked on while he was waiting for a new assistant, but he spent all of his time in this lab with me.

His face didn't show what he thought about Russell. He's not like Ligget, though. Heywood's thoughts are private. Ligget's are hidden. But, every once in a while, while Heywood was working, he'd start to turn around and reach out, or just say 'Jack — ', as if he wanted something, and then he'd catch himself, and his eyes would grow more thoughtful.

I only understood part of what Russell had said that night he was taken away, so I asked Heywood about it yesterday.

'What's the trouble, Pim?' he asked.

'Don't know, for sure. Too much I don't understand about this whole thing. If I knew what some of the words meant, I might not even have a problem.'

'Shoot.'

'Well, it's mostly what Russell was saying, that last night.'

Heywood peeled a strip of skin from his upper lip by catching it between his teeth. 'Yeah.'

'What's a war, or what's war? Soldiers have something to do with it, but what's a soldier? I'm a robot – but why do they want to make more of me? Can I be a soldier and a robot at the same time? Russell kept talking about "they", and the Army, the Air Force, and the Navy. What're they? And are the CIC men the ones who are watching you and each other at the same time?'

Heywood scowled, and grinned ruefully at the same time. 'That's quite a catalogue,' he said. 'And there's even more than that, isn't there, Pimmy?' He put his hand on my side and sort of patted me, the way I'd seen him do with a generator a few times. 'O.K., I'll give you a tape on war and soldiering. That's the next step in the program anyway, and it'll take care of most of those questions.'

'Thanks,' I said. 'But what about the rest of it?'

He leaned against a bench and looked down at the floor. 'Well, "they" are the people who instituted this program – the Secretary of Defense, and the people under him. They all agreed that robot personnel were just what the armed services needed, and they were right. The only trouble is, they couldn't agree among themselves as to what characteristics were desirable in the perfect soldier – or sailor, or airman. They decided that the best thing to do was to come up with a series of different models, and to run tests until they came up with the best one.

'Building you was my own idea. Instead of trying to build prototypes to fit each separate group of specifications, we built one all-purpose model who was, effectively speaking, identical with a human being in almost all respects, with one major difference. By means of cut-offs in every circuit, we can restrict as much of your abilities as we want to, thus being able to modify your general characteristics to fit any one of the various specification groups.

112

We saved a lot of time by doing that, and avoided a terrific nest of difficulties.

'Trouble is, we're using up all the trouble and time we saved. Now that they've got you, they don't want you. Nobody's willing to admit that the only efficient robot soldier is one with all the discretionary powers and individuality of a human being. They can't admit it, because people are afraid of anything that looks like it might be better than they are. And they won't trust what they're afraid of. So, Russell and I had to piddle around with a stupid series of tests. It was a hopeless attempt to come up with something practical that was nevertheless within the limits of the various sets of specifications – which is ridiculous, because there's nothing wrong with you, but there's plenty wrong with the specs. They were designed by people who don't know the first thing about robots or robot thought processes – or the sheer mechanics of thinking, for that matter.'

He shrugged. 'But, they're the people with the authority and the money that's paying for this project – so Jack and I kept puttering, because those were the orders. Knowing that we had the perfect answer all the time, and that nobody would accept it, was what finally got Jack.'

'What about you?' I asked.

He shrugged again. 'I'm just waiting,' he said. 'Eventually they'll either accept you or not. They'll either commend me or fire me, and they might or might not decide it's all my fault if they're not happy. But there's nothing I can do about it, is there? So, I'm waiting.

'Meanwhile, there's the CIC. Actually, that's just a handy label. It happens to be the initials of one of the undercover agencies out of the whole group that infests this place. Every armed service has its own, and I imagine the government has its boys kicking around, too. We just picked one label to cover them all – it's simpler.'

'Russell said they were always watching. But why are they watching each other, too? Why should one armed service be afraid that another's going to get an advantage over it?'

Heywood's mouth moved into a half-amused grin. 'That's

what is known as human psychology, Pimmy. It'll help you to understand it, but if you can't, why, just be glad you haven't got it.'

'Ligget's CIC, you know,' I said. 'Russell accused him of it. He denied it, but if he isn't actually in *the* CIC, then he's in something like it.'

Heywood nodded sourly. 'I know. I wouldn't mind if he had brains enough, in addition, to know one end of a circuit from the other.'

He slapped my side again. 'Pimmy, boy,' he said. 'We're going to have a lot of fun around here in the next few weeks. Yes, sir, a lot of fun.'

August 26, 1974

Ligget was fooling around with me again. He's all right when Heywood's in the lab with me, but when he's alone, he keeps running me through unauthorized tests. What he's doing, actually, is to repeat all the tests Heywood and Russell ran, just to make sure. As long as he doesn't cut out my individuality, I can remember it all, and I guess there was nothing different about the results on any of the tests, because I can tell from his face that he's not finding what he wants.

Well, I hope he tells his bosses that Heywood and Russell were right. Maybe they'll stop this fooling.

Ligget's pretty dumb. After every test, he looks me in the eye and tells me to forget the whole thing. What does he think I am – Trilby?

And I don't understand some of the test performances at all. There *is* something wrong with Ligget.

September 2, 1974

I hadn't realized, until now, that Heywood and Russell hadn't told anyone what they thought about this whole project but, reviewing that tape on war and soldiering, and the way the military mind operates, I can see why nobody would have accepted their explanations.

Ligget caught on to the whole thing today. Heywood came in with a new series of test charts, Ligget took one look at them, and threw them on the table. He sneered at Heywood and said, 'Who do you think you're kidding?'

Heywood looked annoyed and said, 'All right, what's eating you?'

Ligget's face got this hidden crafty look on it. 'How long did you think you could keep this up, Heywood? This test is no different from the ones you were running three years ago. There hasn't been any progress since then, and there's been no attempt to make any. What's your explanation?'

'Uh-huh.' Heywood didn't look particularly worried. 'I was wondering if you were *ever* going to stumble across it.'

Ligget turned mad. 'That attitude won't do you any good. Now, come on, quit stalling. Why were you and Russell sabotaging the project?'

'Oh, stop being such a pompous lamebrain, will you?' Heywood said disgustedly. 'Russell and I weren't doing any sabotaging. We've been following our orders to the last letter. We built the prototype, and we've been testing the various modifications ever since. Anything wrong with that?'

'You've made absolutely no attempt to improve the various modifications. There hasn't been an ounce of progress in this project for the last twenty days.

'Now, look, Heywood' – Ligget's voice became wheedling – 'I can understand that you might have what you'd consider a good reason for all this. What is it – political, or something? Maybe it's your conscience. Don't you *want* to work on something that's eventually going to be applied to war? I wish you'd tell me about it. If I could understand your reasons, it would be that much easier for you. Maybe it's too tough a problem. Is that it, Heywood?'

Heywood's face got red. 'No, it's not. If you think — ' He stopped, dug his fingers at the top of the table, and got control of himself again.

'No,' he said in a quieter, but just as deadly, voice. 'I'm as anxious to produce an artificial soldier as anybody else. And I'm not too stupid for the job, either. If *you* had any brains, you'd see that I already have.'

That hit Ligget between the eyes. 'You have? Where is it, and *why haven't you reported your success?* What is this thing?' He pointed at me. 'Some kind of a decoy?'

Heywood grimaced. 'No, you double-dyed jackass, that's your soldier.'

'What?'

'Sure. Strip those fifteen pounds of cutoffs out of him, redesign his case for whatever kind of ground he's supposed to operate on, feed him the proper tapes, and that's it. The perfect soldier – as smart as any human ever produced, and a hundred times the training and toughness, overnight. Run them out by the thousands. Print your circuits, bed your transistors in silicone rubber, and pour the whole brew into his case. Production difficulties? Watchmaking's harder.'

'*No!*' Ligget's eyes gleamed. 'And I worked on this with you! *Why haven't you reported this!* he repeated.

Heywood looked at him pityingly. 'Haven't you got it through your head? Pimmy's the perfect soldier – all of him, with all his abilities. That includes individuality, curiosity, judgment – and intelligence. Cut one part of that, and he's no good. You've got to take the whole cake, or none at all. One way you starve – and the other way you choke.'

Ligget had gone white. 'You mean, we've got to take the superman – or we don't have anything.'

'Yes, you fumbling jerk!'

Ligget looked thoughtful. He seemed to forget Heywood and me as he stared down at his shoetops. 'They won't go for it,' he muttered. 'Suppose they decide they're better fit to run the world than we are?'

'That's the trouble,' Heywood said. 'They are. They've got everything a human being has, plus incredible toughness and the ability to learn instantaneously. You know what Pimmy did? The day he was assembled, he learned to read and write, after a fashion. How? By listening to me read a paragraph out of a report, recording the sounds, and looking at the report afterwards. He matched the sounds to the letters, recalled what sort of action on Russell's and my part the paragraph had elicited, and sat down behind a typewriter. That's all.'

'They'd junk the whole project before they let something like that run around loose!' The crafty look was hovering at the edges of Ligget's mask again. 'All right, so you've got an answer, but it's not an acceptable one. But why haven't you pushed any of the other lines of investigation?'

'Because there aren't any,' Heywood said disgustedly. 'Any other modification, when worked out to its inherent limits, is worse than useless. You've run enough tests to find out.'

'All right!' Ligget's voice was high. 'Why didn't you report failure, then, instead of keeping on with this shilly-shallying?'

'*Because I haven't failed, you moron!*' Heywood exploded. 'I've got the answer. I've got Pimmy. There's nothing wrong with him – the defect's in the way people are thinking. And I've been going crazy, trying to think of a way to change the people. To hell with modifying the robot! He's as perfect as you'll get within the next five years. It's the people who'll have to change!'

'Uh-huh.' Ligget's voice was careful. 'I see. You've gone as far as you can within the limits of your orders – and you were trying to find a way to exceed them, in order to force the armed services to accept robots like Pimmy.' He pulled out his wallet, and flipped it open. There was a piece of metal fastened to one flap.

'Recognize this, Heywood?'

Heywood nodded.

'All right, then, let's go and talk to a few people.'

Heywood's eyes were cold and brooding again. He shrugged.

The lab door opened, and there was another one of the lab technicians there. 'Go easy, Ligget,' he said. He walked across the lab in rapid strides. His wallet had a different badge in it. 'Listening from next door,' he explained. 'All right, Heywood,' he said, '*I'm* taking you in,' he shouldered Ligget out of the way. 'Why don't you guys learn to stay in your own jurisdiction,' he told him.

Ligget's face turned red, and his fists clenched, but the other man must have had more weight behind him, because he didn't say anything.

Heywood looked over at me, and raised a hand. 'So long, Pimmy,' he said. He and the other man walked out of the lab, with Ligget trailing along behind them. As they got the door open, I saw some other men standing out in the hall. The man who had come into the lab cursed. '*You* guys!' he said savagely. 'This is *my* prisoner, see, and if you think — '

The door closed, and I couldn't hear the rest of what they said, but there was a lot of arguing before I heard the sound of all their footsteps going down the hall in a body.

Well, that's about all, I guess. Except for this other thing. It's about Ligget, and I hear he's not around any more. But you might be interested.

September 4, 1974

I haven't seen Heywood, and I've been alone in the lab all day. But Ligget came in last night. I don't think I'll see Heywood again.

Ligget came in late at night. He looked as though he hadn't slept, and he was very nervous. But he was drunk, too – I don't know where he got the liquor.

He came across the lab floor, his footsteps very loud on the cement, and he put his hands on his hips and looked up at me.

'Well, superman,' he said in a tight, edgy voice, 'you've lost your buddy for good, the dirty traitor. And now you're next. You know what they're going to do to you?' He laughed. 'You'll have lots of time to think it over.'

He paced back and forth in front of me. Then he spun around suddenly and pointed his finger at me. 'Thought you could beat the race of men, huh? Figured you were smarter than we were, didn't you? But we've got you now! You're going to learn that you can't try to fool around with the human animal, because he'll pull you down. He'll claw and kick you until you collapse. That's the way men

118

are, robot. Not steel and circuits – flesh and blood and muscles. Flesh that fought its way out of the sea and out of the jungle, muscle that crushed everything that ever stood in his way, and blood that's spilled for a million years to keep the human race on top. *That's* the kind of an organism *we* are, robot.'

He paced some more and spun again. 'You never had a chance.'

Well, I guess that *is* all. The rest of it, you know about. You can pull the transcriber plug out of here now, I guess. Would somebody say good-bye to Heywood for me – and Russell, too, if that's possible?

COVERING MEMORANDUM,
Blalock, Project Engineer,
to
Hall, Director,
820TH TDRC COMASAMPS

September 21, 1974

Enclosed are the transcriptions of the robot's readings from his memory-bank 'diary', as recorded this morning. The robot is now en route to the Patuxent River, the casting of the concrete block having been completed with the filling of the opening through which the transcription line was run.

As Victor Heywood's successor to the post of Project Engineer, I'd like to point out that the robot was incapable of deceit, and that this transcription, if read at Heywood's trial, will prove that his intentions were definitely not treasonous, and certainly motivated on an honest belief that he was acting in the best interests of the original directive for the project's initiation.

In regard to your Memorandum 8-4792-H of yesterday, a damage report is in process of preparation and will be forwarded to you immediately on its completion.

I fully understand that Heywood's line of research is to be considered closed. Investigations into what Heywood termed the 'zombie' and 'slave' type of robot organization have already begun in an improvised laboratory, and I expect preliminary results within the next ten days.

Preliminary results on the general investigation of other possible types of robot orientation and organization are in copies attached. I'd like to point out that they are extremely discouraging.

(Signed,)

T. E. Blalock, Project Engineer,

820TH TDRC, COMASAMPS

September 25, 1974

PERSONAL LETTER
FROM HALL, DIRECTOR,
820TH TDRC, COMASAMPS,
to
SECRETARY OF DEFENSE
Dear Vinnie,

Well, things are finally starting to settle down out here. You were right, all this place needed was a house-cleaning from top to bottom.

I think we're going to let this Heywood fellow go. We can't prove anything on him – frankly, I don't think there was anything to prove. Russell, of course, is a closed issue. His chance of ever getting out of the hospital is rated at ten per cent.

You know, considering the mess that robot made of the lab, I'd almost be inclined to think that Heywood was right. Can you imagine what a fighter that fellow would have been, if his loyalty had been channeled to some abstract like Freedom, instead of to Heywood? But we can't take the chance. Look at the way the robot's gone amnesic about killing Ligget while he was wrecking the lab. It was something that happened accidentally. It wasn't supposed to happen, so the robot forgot it. Might present difficulties in a war.

So, we've got this Blalock fellow down from M.I.T. He spends too much time talking about Weiner, but he's all right, otherwise.

I'll be down in a couple of days. Appropriations committee meeting. You know how it is. Everybody knows we need the money, but they want to argue about it, first.

Well, that's human nature, I guess.

See you,

Ralph

SUPPLEMENT TO CHARTS:

Menace to Navigation.

Patuxent River, at a point forty-eight miles below Folsom, bearings as below.

Midchannel. Concrete block, 15x15x15. Not dangerous except at extreme low tide.

Go and Behold Them

We spent a long time following bad leads before one finally proved good and we found them. We knew their ship had blown its drive somewhere inside a particular sector of space; it was finding out exactly *where* within that sector that took a long time, and then there was the business of following the faint trail of stray ions from their atmospheric jets. They had used those, knowing they'd be short of fuel for a landing, but concerned, first, with reaching a solar system to crash in. So we followed the trail, blurred as it was by stellar radiation and all the other invisible forces of the universe, and lost it a dozen times before we found them, too late. I'm glad we were too late.

Lew and Norah Harvey were probably the best astrophysics research team the Institute had. There was no question of their being the best-liked. They were young, gay, and unimpressed with their own competence. Norah was a lovely girl, with startling blue eyes set off by her black hair, and a wide, smiling mouth. She was tall, willowy, and graceful. I shall never forget the first time I danced with her, while Lew sat it out with a girl I was squiring about at the time. Norah was light on her feet; like a ballerina, I thought then, but corrected myself. The image is wrong – the frostily graceful, elegant, and perfectly trained figure in its pristine white costume suggests nothing of Norah but the opposite. Norah was warm in my arms – not ethereal at all; yielding, but resilient; light, but full. The qualities of earthiness and youth were perfectly combined in her, so that you knew this was a woman in your arms, and you knew, without a shadow of uncertainty, what a woman was. Her intelligence appealed to your intellect, her youth called to yours, and her femaleness awakened a quality and depth of manhood that you were positive was buried and leached out long ago by the anemic fluid that passes for blood among civilized peoples.

That was Norah. Lew was the quiet one – shorter than Norah by half a centimeter or so, wiry, with a young-old face already full of lines and a pair of brooding, deep-set eyes. He was thoughtful, self-contained, and crammed with a fund of outrageously obscene anecdotes no one but he could have told without vulgarity. Lew had an actor's gift for verisimilitude, and a quiet, deadpan delivery unspoiled by a trace of laughter. He called his little autobiographical stories anecdotes, with the implication that they were true, rather than cleverly constructed and narrated jokes. Perhaps they were. It seemed sometimes that he could never have had time to attend a class in college or, indeed, get the growing young man's necessary minimum of sleep, if all these things had really happened to him.

As a couple, they complemented each other perfectly. Lew was indrawn, Norah was outgoing. Lew loved her with a quiet intensity that came close to desperation. The look was there in his eyes, though it had to be watched for. Norah loved him with effusive generosity.

I have said they were probably the best research team the Institute had. They were. Lew was an astrophysicist with a D.Sc. after his name. Norah was a metrographic engineer and statistical analyst. Neither her gaiety nor Lew's story-telling had anything to do with their ability to take out a research ship, spend six months alone in it while they drifted about in the deeps of an interstellar dust cloud, and come back with half again as much data as the next team. Or perhaps they did – I don't know. Whenever anyone at the Institute remarked on it, Lew would drawl in his non-committal way: 'Well, there's no room in one of those cans for a dance floor. So we might as well work.'

We always thought that was one of Lew's most quotable lines. Most research teams are made up of what are called 'young marrieds' by the people who sell saccharine for a living, and you can imagine for yourself what kind of repartee that could give rise to at an Institute staff party.

We had those parties often enough. Six months in isolation made us all yearn for as much in the way of noise and crowds of people as could be mustered, and the mustering process had been evolved to a point of high efficiency. Every homecoming team found itself welcomed royally, and every outgoing team had a day or two of grace after the socializing before the Institute medical staff would certify their metabolisms fit for service again. We were a feast-and-famine group, a close-knit academic cadre with few ties outside the clan and little desire for them. Most of us were married. Those who weren't were usually as good as, and two by two we formed our questing brotherhood, as Lew Harvey put it once.

We lost very few to the impersonal dangers of the universe. When Lew and Norah disappeared, it was a stab in all our hearts. Even the Board of Trustees in charge of the research program, instructed to act with Olympian detachment in promulgating its success, managed to bend a little: it found an extra appropriation at just that time to finance the sending of ten ships into space simultaneously. The official purpose was to accelerate the program, and thus increase Man's knowledge of the universe so much more quickly, of course – but somehow it was made plain to those of us who went that if we did not bring much routine data, that would be considered only a natural hiatus in the always unsteady curve of human progress.

So we stripped the recording instruments out of the ships and made room for a relief observer, and his extra complement of food and air. It was tricky, but it meant we could stay out searching a little longer, and be a little more alert. So equipped, we left the Institute far behind and converged on the sector where the Harveys had been – a sector only a hundred light-years deep, containing an estimated more hundred thousand bodies where their ship might have crashed. And we began to search.

We found them; *my* ship found them, that is. And much too late. We couldn't have saved Lew if we had known the exact pinpointed spot to go to – not if we had had the wings of angels. But we might have saved Norah, with a little luck. I'm glad for both of them that we didn't.

What we found was a rogue body where nothing had any business being. It was forging blindly through the deep – sunless, perhaps a thousand miles in diameter, and the mass readings were fluctuating wildly as we came near. Dozzen, the extra on my team, showed me the figures. He was very young. Cleancut, handsome – fresh fish, and unassigned as yet when the emergency had come up.

'The machines have dropped a stitch, Harry,' he said. 'Look at these – new mass readings every thousand miles as we come closer.'

I looked at them and grunted. 'No. The readings are right.'

'Oh, come on now, Harry – how could they be?'

'If a gravitic generator were buried in the heart of that body.'

'Gravitic *generator*! My left-footed aunt, Harry.'

I can't say I ever cared for loudly positive people. I winced and tapped the other readings scribbled down on the scratch pad. 'Just because nobody's ever seen it before, never say what you're looking at isn't there.' I could have launched into my favorite diatribe on explorers who resisted making discoveries, but what was the use? 'Look at these: Atmosphere one hundred percent inert gases, mostly neon. Furthermore, it's fluorescing. Hardly a likely state of affairs in nature. You will also notice the presence of some neon snow on the ground, but not much. But the mean temperature is down nudging absolute zero. Why isn't *all* of that atmosphere piled up in drifts? I'd say the reason is that it *was,* until very recently – that something, like a spaceship crash on the surface, activated a series of machines which are busily raising the temperature and otherwise moving the ecology from a dormant to an active state. I doubt if Nature includes that kind of reaction when it constructs a planetoid. I'd say that whole business down there might be a machine – or, rather, a complex of mechanisms with some particular purpose in view.'

He looked at me as if I were crazy. I looked at him as if he were being deliberately stupid. Some day, an expedition equipped with recorders instead of our ship's simple analyzers, is going to have to go out there and prove one of us right. I don't wish to be on that expedition. Dozzen can go, if he wants to. I wish him joy of it.

Whatever it was – natural anomaly or artificial leftover from a day and people I am glad are gone – we landed there, coming down on a relatively flat place in the vicious terrain. The sky flamed yellow above us and its fluorescence might have been a working light for autonomous machines, long since gone. It is impossible to speculate on the history of the place; I say, again, that it would be a mistake to go there and try. And for all I know, it was entirely different in appearance as recently as when Lew and Norah Harvey's ship came hurtling out of the sky and smashed itself like a bug on a windscreen. But if anything endowed with biological life ever lived in that place as we saw it, I have only horror for that thing.

What we saw was Hell; all about us, boundless and bare, were scarps and ridges of bleak, decayed metal so desolate, so pitilessly torn and twisted into razor edged shapes that for a moment I seriously expected to hear a scream of agony from the swirling air.

There was light. There was no heat. The incredible chill of the place was sucking at our ship already; the cabin heaters were whirring furiously. We shivered as we peered out through the windows and outraged our eyes with that masochist's landscape.

Not all of Nature's forms are beautiful – even a dedicated research man occasionally has his soul intruded upon by some particularly offensive example. But all of them, even the most revolting, have a certain organic rightness to them. One can see the reasonableness, if not accept the architectural style, of every form the universe erects.

Not this place. If you have seen a tin can left to rust for a year, its walls broken down and flaking away, then you have seen something of the contours that metallic landscape took, but only something. If you have seen a giant meteorite; pitted, burnt, leprous, half-molten and congealed in gobbets, barely suggestive of some other shape now lost

126

that might once have been regular and purposeful, then you have experienced some of the feeling that place gave us. But not much of it.

The Harveys' broken ship made an island of sanity in that place. It was smashed and scattered, but its fragments, pieced together, would have made a whole.

We could land nowhere near it. We put our own ship down six miles away. We stood at the ports, looking out, and finally I said: 'We have to go out.'

Doris, my regular team mate, said: 'I'll get the suits.' She got all three. In the backs of all our minds, I think, was an irrational fear that something might happen to the ship while we were all gone. But there was an even greater fear of being separated in that place, and, to avoid that, we were immediately willing to chance being marooned. We were not very sane in our decision, but in that savage place the nerves were much more potent than the intellect. So we locked our suits on and, armored against any external fearsomeness, clambered down the ladder.

'This way,' I said, looking at my direction finder. and set off across the terrain. I tried to look only straight ahead. Doris and Dozzen followed me, at some small distance, staying close to each other. I envied them, for I was very much alone.

I had expected that Doris would find better company than me. It was not a new experience for me to lose my team mate, though it had never before happened in my immediate presence. If Norah and Lew were known for their constancy, I was known for my lack of it. One, perhaps two trips were as long as I and my team mate of the moment ever lasted. If there had been something spectacular or particularly noteworthy in my many partings, the board of directors would long since have removed me. But they were only quiet, amicable dissolutions of temporary working partnerships. No one found them scandalous, though juicy gossip was as well received by the Institute staff as it is anywhere. Each new occurrence was simply another example of Harry Becker's not having found the right girl – or of the girl's not having found the right man in Harry Becker.

Good old Harry Becker, decent fellow, nothing wrong, fine companion – on all levels, one might add – but apparently just not the right man for Doris; or Sylvia, or Joan, or Ellen, or Rosemary . . .

'Harry!' I was inching around a jagged wave of pitted metal, and Doris's cry in my headphones almost sent me stumbling against a razor edge. I caught my balance, and turned. Doris had shrunk back against Dozzen.

'Harry, I saw something . . .' Her voice trailed away. 'Oh – no, no, I didn't.' She laughed weakly in embarrassment. 'You'll have to forgive my girlish jumpiness. It's that formation over to your right – for a minute there, it looked like an animal of some kind. I only saw it out of the corner of my eye, and I played a little trick on myself.' She made her voice light, but she was shaken.

I looked around, and said nothing. It was Dozzen who put into words what I had seen and been trying to avoid. Our nerves were taut enough. But Dozzen said it anyway: 'There's another. And some more over there. The place is crawling with them. It looks like a lunatic's zoo.'

It did. It did, and it was nothing to try to be matter-of-fact about – not then, not ever.

Now that we were down in it, the terrain assumed individual features. I wished it hadn't, for it had become evident what those features were.

Beasts prowled around us; frozen forever, but prowling. unfinished, mis-shapen, terribly mangled, they bared their teeth and claws at us, only to become tortured metal as we looked at them directly. We saw them beside and a little behind us, always, and not only beasts, but the cities and dwellings they had overrun – the homes they had gutted, the streets they had littered with the remains of their prey. We walked on among them and they followed us, always at the corners of our eyes, and when we turned to see them better they were gone, to lurk where we had been looking.

'It's a common form of illusion,' Dozzen said weakly.

'Yes,' I said, and led the way through their gauntlet.

'This is a terrible place,' Doris said.

It was.

We reached the crashed ship, and Dozzen said: 'Look!'

The ship lay mashed, but a hull section had held together. There were weld scars on it. Perhaps it had not survived the crash whole, but it was airtight now. There was a cairn beside it, with a cross welded together out of structural members atop it.

'Which one?' I thought. *'Which one?'* and leaped clambering over the ridges and heaps of fused metals, panting with urgency. I ran at the cairn and flung myself up it, and sprawled at the foot of the cross to read in bright scratches: 'Lewis Harvey, Explorer.' I slid down the cairn in a shower of fragments, and pounded on the sealed hull section hatch, shouting 'Norah! Norah! *Norah!*' until Doris and Dozzen came and pulled me gently away.

They cut open the door while I sat facing away. They had looked in the port and seen her lying still in her suit; I could not have done either. And once inside, it was they who picked her up tenderly and laid her down on the bunk, the suit out of power, the inside of the faceplate frosted over, and the suit limp, limp and boneless – almost – but too heavy to be empty, though the stupid hope came to me.

They rigged power lines from their suits to the report recorder we found set up beside where she had fallen, and lines back into our audio circuits, and when I heard her voice I did not make a sound.

'Last report,' it said in her voice, exhausted and labouring. 'Power going fast. I'm in my suit now, and when that goes, that'll be it.

'I don't know where we are. Whatever this place is, it must have just drifted into this sector. I don't know what it was – what purpose a race would have for a machine like this.' She stopped momentarily, and the breath she drew was a gasp. I thought of her, starving for air, starving for heat, broken by the crash as she must have been, and I remembered again, the first night she had danced in my arms.

'The changes outside are still going on,' she resumed.

'But much more slowly. I think they'll stop soon. I see them try, try to complete themselves, and fail, and stop, and start again. But they are slowing down, and each attempt is less forceful than the last. I wish I could understand what was causing them.

'I wish Lew were here,' she said wistfully. And there was no question now whether she had given up hope or not. She began to speak for a record greater than the Institute's.

'I loved you, Lew,' she said quietly and serenely. 'Even though you never believed me. Even though sometimes you hated me. I loved you. If I could never prove it to you in that one narrow way, still, I loved you.' Her voice was growing very faint. 'I hope I shall meet you,' she said. 'And if I do, then I would like these to be the first words I say to you: I love you.'

That was all. She was dead. Doris reached over and pulled the audio line out of our suits.

There was a long silence. Finally Dozzen sighed and said: 'I don't suppose that will mean much to anyone. There are probably earlier spools in the recorder, from when she was still thinking clearly.'

'Probably,' I said. Doris was watching me closely. I looked at her and thought I had never been as clever as I thought I had – nor as clever at hiding myself from women as I had been at hiding from myself.

I went over to the bunk and picked up Norah in my arms, and carried her outside. Dozzen may have tried to follow me. If he did, Doris held him back. I was left alone.

I built the new cairn beside the other, and welded a new cross with the tools we all carried in our suits, and etched her name upon it. I had plucked the lumps of toothed metal one by one from the surface of the machine-world, and piled them carefully, and opened her faceplate so that the inert atmosphere could flood in, wash out the trapped carbon dioxide and the last trickles of oxygen, and leave her ageless, perfect forever, frozen.

I was done at last, and came down from the cairn. Doris was waiting for me. She took my arm and touched helmets with me so Dozzen could not hear. She said:

'Harry – it's often the most feminine women who . . .'

'Who aren't female at all?'

'That's a terrible way to put it,' she answered softly. 'I wonder if that's the way Lew thought of it – if he tortured himself out of shape inside, because he chose the cruelest way of thinking of it? You knew Norah – she was warm, and friendly, and a wonderful person. Who can say, now, what may or may not have happened when she was just becoming a woman? If Lew thought she was a living lie, he ought to have thought that perhaps she knew she was lying to herself, as well. If he'd ever thought to be kind . . .'

'Don't tell *me* these things!' I said bitterly, instantly sorry. '*I* wasn't married to her.'

'Are you sorry or glad, Harry?' she asked quietly.

I didn't know, then.

It was while we were on our way back to the ship that Doris touched my arm again. 'Harry . . . *look!*'

I raised my head, and the beasts of the place were gone.

It was a subtle change – a shift of planes, a movement of curvatures; no more than that – not yet. We never stayed to see the end of that process. It was moving too quickly for us to endure.

The snow stopped and the snow on the ground burst into curling vapor that shrouded us in sparkling mist, as though Spring had come into this place at last.

The metal shapes were still molten, their outlines still broken, and they were still metal, still cold and hard. But the beasts were gone – the pent-up nightmares of frustration were lost with even that beginning of a change. Everywhere the corners of our eyes could see, there was striving. The illusions, Dozzen would have said – did say, the fool – were softening, turning into calm, friendly shapes. The raw hatred had gone, and the viciousness. Now there were spires, minarets, the fragile battlements of faerie cities, and here were hedges, trees, and there – *I* saw it, if Dozzen did not and Doris never spoke of it – I saw two lovers with their arms entwined.

'It's turning beautiful!' Doris said. It was. It was wild, eerie – many things; not all of them, perhaps, as wispily graceful as the best beauticians would have them – but it was vibrantly alive, glorious with growth.

We left it quickly. There was that about it which unsettled Dozzen badly, and made Doris moody. It did many things to me.

Dozzen made the formal report, without benefit of the recorders and analyzers that would have made fallible human impressions unnecessary. Doris and I initialled it, and I will never know if she, in her own way, was being as evasive as I. We have never talked about it, because what is there to ask?

Illusions are subjective phenomena, and no two people can possibly be expected to see the same face in a shifting cloud, nor can one see anything but the lion in the jumbled granite mountainside where another insists he sees a sheep. These things are nothing but reflections of the viewer's self. How can they possibly be measured or compared?

Dozzen's report says the terrain of the place is broken into free forms which the mind readily supplies with familiar shapes, in a search for the familiar where the familiar does not, in fact, exist. That is as far as he will go, on paper, though he knows there is enough more to the truth to make him unhappy. But he knows he doesn't know just where that truth might lie, so he will not push himself beyond the point where he feels safe.

I think *I* know what a machine of planetary dimensions might be intended to do, though I cannot picture a race which would choose metal in an inert atmosphere for a medium in which to attempt the creation of life.

I think that is what we found. I think all races must come to it someday in the prime of their greatness. I think the race that built this machine failed, and died, or we would not be here today. But I think that race came very, very close when it launched its machine into space, a messenger and vessel of nearly fruitful hope. I think they may have missed only one ingredient of life, even though they chose so strange a thing as metal for its womb.

I think I know why the snow was falling again when we first came there. Norah buried Lew, and not in his suit, for that was still hanging in its locker. And when she buried Lew, the planet-machine began to stir to movement again, and take to itself what it had always lacked and, lacking, almost died. And now, having that thing – that spark – it began to change – to search after its goal once more, to strive, to fail, but trying, trying nonetheless, with all it could get from Lew Harvey. And failing, and going back into its ageless somnolence again, leaving only its half-successful attempts behind it to haunt us when we landed. For whatever it was that unfulfilled, tortured Lew Harvey yielded up in the crash, Lew Harvey was not enough.

And I do not say that a Mark Four suit will trap and restrain the kind of thing required for the creation of life . . . or that a dead girl can say *I love you*. But the snow stopped after I opened Norah's suit, and the beasts departed. And I saw movement in that planet's metal, at the last. I don't think it was a trick of the light, or of the evaporating snow.

I think, someday, when Doris and I are out there again, we shall meet something. I think she thinks so too, though we never speak of it or plan for it, because no planning is possible.

I wonder, sometimes, if that primordial race, so great, could be so thoughtless, ever, as to fail – if greater plans were made than I am quite ready to believe. I hope not. I would rather believe that blind chance was the catalyst. In that belief, there is a kind of hope.

I am afraid, and proud, and troubled. I think of what might have been if Norah had loved me, if Lew Harvey had not met her before I ever knew them. I think of the thing between them, the thing we never suspected and they never betrayed. I am glad for them now, if I am sometimes terrified for the universe of Man:

For I think that someday, in the deeps we sift, we shall meet Lew and Norah Harvey's children.

The Executioner

Late in the morning, just before noon, Samson Joyce sat in a folding chair placed behind the high, granite judges' bench which faced the plaza. In a few minutes, he would be climbing up the steps of the bench to its top, where he would stand behind the solid parapet and look down at the Accused's box in the plaza. Now he was checking his gun.

He worked the slide, watching the breech open and the extractor reach with its metal fingertip. The bolt drew back; hesitated; jumped forward. He took out a silk rag and wiped off the excess oil, spreading it in a thin, uniform film over the metal. He thumbed the cartridges out of the clip, oiled the clip action, and reloaded. He did all this with patient care and long practice.

The sun had been breaking in and out of clouds all morning, and there was a fitful wind. The pennants and family standards around the plaza were twisting restlessly. It was an uncertain day.

The gun was his old favorite; a gas-operated 15-millimeter Grennell that had been with him since his old days as Associate Justice of Utica. It fitted comfortably into his hand, as well it might after all these years. It was not the jeweled, plated and engraved antique they expected him to use at the big trials in New York City or Buffalo. It was just a gun; it did what it was meant for, cleanly and efficiently, and he used it whenever he could. It didn't pretend to be more than it was. It never failed.

He scowled, looking down at it. He scowled at feelings he knew were foolish and wished he did not have.

Once he'd been in his twenties, looking forward. Now he was a shade past fifty, and what he looked back on was subtly less satisfactory than what he had looked forward to.

He raised his head and looked at the three men who were his Associate Justices today, as they walked toward him from the hotel. Blanding, with his brief case, Pedersen, with his brief case, and Kallimer with his frown.

Joyce's heavy lower lips tightened in a fleeting touch of amusement that slackened and was gone without a trace. All of them were younger than he'd been at Utica, and all three were farther along. Blanding was the Associate Justice here in Nyack, which meant his next appointment would take him out of the suburbs and into the city proper. Pedersen was waiting for the results of the Manhattan by-election to be officially confirmed. When they were, he'd take his seat in the Legislature. And Kallimer was Special Associate Justice to the Chief Justice of Sovereign New York, Mr Justice Samson Ezra Joyce. Perhaps it was the strain of remembering his full title that gave him the permanent frown, drawing his thin eyebrows closer together and pinching the bridge of his bony nose. Or perhaps he was rehearsing the sound of 'Chief Justice of Sovereign New York, Mr Justice Ethan Benoni Kallimer.'

All three of them were fortunate young men, in the early flower of their careers. But, being young men, they were not quite capable of enjoying their good fortune. Joyce could guess what they must be feeling as they walked toward him.

They'd be thinking Joyce was a crusty old fool who was hopelessly conservative in his administration of Justice – that younger men were more capable.

They'd be thinking he wanted to live forever, without giving someone else a chance. They were sure he thought he was the only one fit to wear a Chief Justice's Trial Suit.

And they called him Old Knock-Knees whenever they saw him in his Suit tights.

Every trial saw them with their brief cases, each with its gun inside. Each of them waited for the day The Messire reversed Joyce's human and, therefore, fallible verdict. There'd be a new Chief Justice needed for the next trial, and promotions all along the line.

He worked the Bogen slide again, nodded with satisfaction, and replaced the clip. In the thirty years since he'd begun. The Messire had not reversed his verdicts. He had come close – Joyce had scars enough – but, in the end, he'd done no more than raise a formal objection, as it were, before substantiating Joyce's decisions.

Blanding, Pedersen, and Kallimer, in their plain, unfigured black vests, the stark white lace frothing at their wrists, stopped in front of him.

Somber men. Jealous men – even Pedersen, who was leaving the bench. Impatient men.

Joyce put away his gun. Young men, who failed to realize their good fortune in still having a goal to attain, and a dream to fulfill. Who did not foresee that it was the men at the top – the men who had reached the goal – who had to dedicate themselves unceasingly to the preservation of the ideal; who, with the Messire's help, laboured each minute of their lives to keep the purpose of their lives untarnished. The young men never knew, until they reached the top, that the joy was in the struggle, and the drudgery in the maintenance of the victory. The young men served the ideal, without a thought to wondering what kept the ideal high and firm in its purpose.

Some day, they might learn.

'Good morning, Justice,' almost in chorus.

'Good morning, Justices. I imagine you slept well?'

From the sound of the spectators, he judged that the Accused had just been brought into the plaza. It was interesting to note the change in crowd voices over the years. Lately, it had been easy to differentiate between the sound from the family boxes and the noise of the people, which was a full octave lower.

Joyce looked up at the plaza tower clock. A few moments remained.

Dissatisfaction? Was that what he felt?

He imagined himself trying to explain what he felt to one of these youngsters, and – yes – 'dissatisfaction' was the word he would use.

But that wouldn't ever happen. Blanding was too young

136

to do anything but sneer at the knock-kneed old fool with his swollen ankles. Pedersen was out of it. And Kallimer, of course, whose intelligence he respected, was too intelligent to listen. He had his own ideas.

Joyce stood up. Touched the figure of The Messire buried under his neckpiece, straightened the hang of his vest, adjusted his wig, and turned toward his Associates. In so doing, he allowed his glance to quickly sweep over the Accused for the first time. She was standing in her box, waiting. Just one glance, before she could realize he'd compromised his dignity by looking at her.

'Well, Justices, it's time.'

He waited to follow them up the steps which would be hard on his ankles.

First, Blanding had to relinquish his right to try the case, since it was in his jurisdiction.

Joyce, standing by himself on the higher central section of the platform, leaned forward slightly until his thighs were pressed against the cool stone of the bench's back. It took some of the weight off his ankles.

No one would notice it from the plaza below. Looking up at the bluff gray walls of the bench's face, all anyone could see were the torsos of four men; two in black, then one standing somewhat taller in his brilliant Suit, and then another in black. That last was Blanding, and now he stepped around the end of the bench, forward onto the overhanging slab that was the bailiff's rostrum at ordinary trials, and stopped, slim, motionless, and black, standing out over the plaza below.

Joyce was grateful for the breeze. The Suit was heavy with its embroidered encrustations, and the thick collar, together with his neckpiece, was already making him perspire. Still and all, he did not regret coming here to Nyack. In New York and Buffalo, his trials were ostentatious ceremonials, overrun with minor functionaries and elaborate protocol toward the First Families. Here in Nyack, there were no functionaries and no First Families. The ceremony of trial could be stripped down to its simple but beautiful essentials. Blanding would handle the statements of charges. Pedersen would keep track, and Kallimer . . .

Kallimer would wait to see whether The Messire approved.

Joyce looked down at the crowd. Scarlet, gold, and azure blue struck his eyes from the family boxes. He saw the flash of light on rings and earrings, the soft, warm color of the ladies' wimples.

The people were a dun mass, dressed in the dark, subdued colors they had been affecting lately. Joyce reflected that, without their contrast, the family members might not appear so brilliant in their boxes. But that was only a hasty digression, fluttering across his mind like an uneasy bird at sunset.

He understood from Blanding that the people had some unusual interest in this trial. Looking down, he could see the crowd was large.

Joyce plainly heard Blanding draw breath before he began to speak. When he did, he spoke slowly, and the acoustic amplifiers inside the stone bench made his voice grave and sonorous.

'People of Nyack — '

The crowd became absolutely still, all of them watching the straight, motionless black figure standing above them.

This was justice, Joyce thought as he always did when a trial began, the mood slipping over him. This was the personification of the ideal. The straight, unbending figure; the grave voice.

'The Nyack Court of Common Justice, of Sovereign New York, is now in Session.'

He disliked Blanding, Joyce reflected, watching the Associate half-turn and extend an arm toward him. He disliked Pedersen, and Kallimer made him uneasy. But they were together in this. This was above personality, and above humanity. The Messire, the four of them, the families and the people; together, what they did here today was their bond and heritage. This was their bulwark against savagery.

Blanding had held the gesture just long enough. 'Mr

Justice Joyce, Chief Justice of Sovereign New York, Presiding.'

There was a burst of excited applause from the families. They'd expected him to preside at a trial of this nature, of course, but they were excited now, nevertheless. This was the official stamp. This was the recognition of their importance, and of the importance of this case. Joyce bowed his head in acknowledgment.

'Mr Justice Kallimer, Chief Associate Justice.'

Joyce noted that Kallimer's applause was much more sparse. But then, he had almost no reputation here. He'd originally come from Waverly, which was far across the nation at the Pennsylvania border. He'd been noticed by the Bar Association, but until he'd presided at some trials in the Hudson area, very few people would recognize his name.

'Mr Justice Pedersen, Recording Justice.'

Pedersen drew a better hand than Kallimer. That was because he was a New York City judge.

Joyce did not permit his thin smile to touch his face. For all of that, it was Kallimer who would succeed him, even if Pedersen had stayed on the bench. Kallimer was not a crowd-pleaser, but he had been efficient in Waverly, and he could be efficient here, too, if he had to.

Joyce waited for the proper amount of expectant silence to accumulate. Then he raised his head.

'Let trial begin.'

There was a fresh burst of applause. When it subsided, he turned to Blanding. 'Justice Blanding will state the case.' Joyce's tone, too, was deep and majestic. Part of that was the amplifiers, doing their invisible work within the bench, but part of it was in him, his back stiffening and his ankles taking his full weight. His head was erect, and he felt his slow pulse moving regularly through his veins, beating with the gratification of the act of trial.

Blanding looked down at the Accused's box.

'The case of John Doe in complaint against Clarissa

139

Jones. The concurrent case of the People of Sovereign New York against Clarissa Jones.'

Joyce could now look at the Accused. She was obviously in poor control of herself, gripping the railing before her with tight hands. Then he turned toward Pedersen.

'Justice Pedersen, what has been the progress of this case?'

'Mr Justice, the complaint of John Doe has been withdrawn in cognizance of the superior claim of the People.'

That was ritual, too. Once the attention of Justice had been drawn to the crime, the original complainant withdrew. Otherwise, the name of the complaining family member would have had to be revealed in open court.

Joyce turned back toward Blanding.

'Justice Blanding will proceed with the statement of the People's case.'

Blanding paused for another breath. 'We, the People of Sovereign New York, accuse Clarissa Jones of attempting to usurp a place not her own; of deliberately and maliciously using the wiles of her sex to claim recognition from a member of a family, said family member being of minor age and hereinafter designated as 'John Doe'. We further accuse Clarissa Jones, People's woman, of fomenting anarchy — '

The indictment continued. Joyce watched the Accused's face, noting that despite her emotional strain, she at least retained sufficient propriety not to interrupt with useless exclamations or gestures. The girl had some steel in her, somewhere. He was pleased at her restraint; interruptions destroyed the rhythm of Trial. She'd have her chance to appeal.

He turned to Pedersen with an inquiring lift of his eyebrows. Pedersen moved closer, keeping his mouth carefully out of the pickup area.

'The girl was young Normandy's mistress. He's got a summer lodge on the river, here,' he whispered.

'Joshua Normandy's boy?' Joyce asked in some surprise.

'That's right.' Pedersen grimaced. 'He might have been

more astute, and investigated her a little. She's got a number of relatives in the local craft guilds and whatnot.'

Joyce frowned. 'Illegitimate relationships don't mean anything.'

Pedersen shrugged the shoulder away from the crowd. 'Legally, no. But in practice the People have taken to recognizing these things among themselves. I understand their couples refer to each other as husband and wife when among groups of their own kind. I know that's of no weight in court,' he went on hastily, 'but the girl's apparently an aristocrat among them. It could be natural for her to assume certain privileges. Normandy's specific complaint was that she came up to him on a public street and addressed him by his first name. Well, there she was going a little too far.'

Pedersen hooked his mouth into a knowing smile.

'Yes,' Joyce answered sharply, his cheeks flattening with rage, as he looked down at the Accused. 'She was.'

The youngsters didn't yet understand. They could smile at it. Joyce couldn't. The fact that this was just a thoughtless girl in love made no difference. What had to be judged here was the legal situation, not the human emotions involved.

Centuries ago, The Messire had established this society, speaking through his prophets, and it was that society which Joyce defended here, just as hundreds of Justices defended it every day throughout the land.

There were those worthy of marriage, and those who were not. Those with the mental capacity to rule, administer, judge, and choose the sick to be healed, and those without it. The notion had long ago been exploded that all human beings were equal.

The blunt facts of life were that talent and mental capacity were hereditary. Some human beings were better equipped than others to judge what was best for the human race as a whole, but, with unrestricted marriage, these superior qualities were in grave danger of dilution.

To have attempted to breed the ordinary people out of

141

existence would have been impossible. The sea is not dried up with blotting paper. But the building of dikes *was* possible.

Out of the rubble and flame of the Twenty-first Century, The Messire had handed down the answer, and the Law. The Law was the dike that penned the sea of ordinary people away from the wellsprings of the families.

Through His prophets, The Messire had ordained his First Families, and they, in turn, had chosen others. To all of these were given the sacrament of marriage and the heritage of name and property for their children. For centuries, the families had been preserved, their members choosing wives and husbands only out of their own kind.

It was unnecessary to enforce childlessness on the remaining people. Neither superior intelligence nor talent were required for the world's routine work.

Nor had 'enforcement', as such, of The Messire's Law been required for many years, now. It was not that the people were impious or heretical. Rather it was that, being human, they were prone to error. In their untutored minds, the purpose and meaning of the Law sometimes became unclear.

Despite that simple piety, if young Normandy had been even more of a fool, and let the incident pass, some members of the people might mistakenly have felt such behavior was permissible. The precedent would have been established. If, after that, some other error had been allowed to go uncorrected, yet another step away from the Law might be taken. And after that, another —

Anarchy. And the widening erosion in the dike.

Joyce scowled down at the Accused. He only wished it hadn't been a girl.

Blanding reached the end of his indictment and paused, with a gesture to Joyce.

Joyce looked down at the Accused again, partly because he wished to study her again and partly because it lent weight to his opinion.

The girl's trembling confirmed his previous tentative

142

decision. There was no purpose in dragging this on. The quickest conclusion was the best.

'Thank you, Justice,' he said to Blanding. He addressed the Accused.

'Young woman, we have heard your indictment. Justice Blanding will now repeat the etiquette of Trial, in order that there may be no doubt in your mind of your rights.'

'The Messire is your judge,' Blanding told her gravely. 'The verdict we deliver here is not conclusive. If you wish to appeal, make your appeal to Him.'

There was a stir and rustle in the crowd, as there always was. Joyce saw a number of people touch the images at their throats.

'We shall deliberate on this verdict, each separately determining the degree of your guilt. When we have reached a verdict, our separate opinions shall determine the degree of mundane appeal granted you.'

Joyce threw a quick glance at the girl. She was looking up at Blanding with her hands on the rail of her box, her arms stiffly extended.

'If your case has been misrepresented to this Court, The Messire will intervene in your behalf. If you are innocent, you have nothing to fear.'

Having completed the recital, he stopped and looked out over the heads of the crowd.

Joyce stepped back, and saw that Kallimer and Pedersen were looking down at his hands, hidden from the crowd. He signaled for a verdict of 'Completely Guilty'. Giving the girl a weapon to defend herself would be ridiculous. If she succeeded in firing at all, she was sure to miss him and injure someone in the crowd. It was best to get this case out of the way quickly and efficiently. The thing had to be squashed right here.

To his surprise, he saw Kallimer signal back 'reconsider'.

Joyce looked at the Associate. He might have expected something of the sort from Blanding, but a man of Kallimer's intelligence should have arrived at the proper conclusion.

Perhaps the Bar Association had been very wise to give

him this trial, instead of letting some lesser Justice handle it. He'd had his doubts, but this wiped them out.

Without looking at Kallimer, but letting him plainly see the angry swell of the set jaw muscle that tightened his cheek, Joyce signaled 'imperative!'

Kallimer sighed inaudibly, and his 'acquiesce' was limp-fingers, as though he were trying to convey resignation, as well.

Joyce faced front, still furious, but with his voice under control.

'Justice Blanding, have you reached a verdict?' He moved his left shoulder slightly.

Blanding, from his position on the rostrum, turned and saw the signal.

'I find the Accused completely guilty, Mr Justice,' he said.

Joyce turned to Pedersen in the absolute silence that always fell over a plaza during the rendering of the verdict.

'Completely guilty, Mr Justice.'

Joyce turned to Kallimer.

The man's lips twitched in a faint, sardonic smile. 'Completely guilty, Mr Justice.'

Joyce looked down at the Accused. 'I also find you completely guilty as charged,' he said. 'You will not be allowed a weapon with which to make mundane appeal. Your only recourse is to The Messire's mercy. I pray that our verdict is correct.'

He stepped back to a new outburst of applause from the family boxes, satisfied that he had done his best. So far, it was a good trial. Even Kallimer's rebelliousness had been evident only here on the bench. The majesty and unanimity of justice had been preserved as far as the crowd could tell.

He turned and walked slowly down the platform steps, through the deep hush that locked the plaza.

It *had* been a good trial. The Bar Association would detail it and its significance in the Closed Archives, and, generations from now, the older Justices would be reading about it, seeing how his action today had choked off the incipient attack on this culture and this civilization.

But that was not uppermost in Joyce's mind. What men a hundred years from now would say could not have much personal significance to him. What made his pulse beat more and more strongly as he descended the steps, turned the corner of the bench, and walked out into the plaza, was the knowledge that his contemporaries – the other Justices of the Bar Association – the men who had also come to the top, and who understood what the burden was – would know he had not failed the ideal.

He stopped just short of the Ground of Trial and gestured to the attendants around the Accused. They removed the Accused's clothing to guard against armor or concealed weapons, and stepped aside.

Joyce took the final stride that placed him on the Justice's Square, where other amplifiers once more took up his voice.

'The Accused will come forward to make her appeal.'

The girl stumbled a bit coming out of the box, and he heard a slight sound of disappointment from the family boxes. It was not a good Entrance. But that could be forgotten.

He reached down, and the gun slipped out of its holster in one smooth sweep of his arm that was pure line of motion as he simultaneously half-turned, his vest standing out in a perfect straight-up-and-down cylindrical fall from his neck to its hem. He came up slightly on his toes, and there was a scattering of 'bravo!' from the family boxes as well as the more reserved 'excellent' which was really all a lame man deserved for his draw, no matter how perfect his arm motion.

The Accused was standing, pale of face, in the Square of Appeal.

Holding his draw, Joyce waited to speak the ultimate sentence.

He was growing old. The number of trials remaining to him was low. Some day soon, on a verdict of 'probably

145

guilty', perhaps, when the Accused had a fully loaded weapon, The Messire would reverse the verdict.

Not because of his physical slowness. The lameness and hitch in the draw would be merely symptomatic of his advancing slowness of mind. He would not have interpreted the case correctly.

He knew that, expected it, and felt only acceptance for it. A Justice who rendered an incorrect verdict deserved the penalty just as much as a guilty member of the people.

Meanwhile, this was the upheld ideal.

'You have been adjudged completely guilty as charged,' he said, listening to the old words roll out over the plaza. 'You have not been granted pardon by this Court. Make your appeal to The Messire.'

The Accused looked at him wide-eyed out of her pallor. There was no certainty she was praying, but Joyce presumed she was.

Justice rested in The Messire. He knew the guilty and the innocent; punished the one and protected the other. Joyce was only His instrument, and Trial was only the opportunity for His judgment to become apparent. Men could judge each other, and pass sentence. But men could be wise or foolish in their decisions. That was the fallible nature of Man.

Here was where the test came; here where the Accused prayed to The Messire for the ultimate, infallible judgment. This was Trial.

His finger tightened on the trigger while his arm came slowly down and forward. This, too, was where Joyce prayed to the Ultimate Judge, asking whether he had done wisely, whether he had once more done well. Each trial was his Trial, too. This was his contact with The Messire. This was Truth.

Something whirled out of the silent crowd of people and landed at the girl's feet. It was a gun, and the girl scrambled for it.

As soon as she picked it up, Joyce knew he'd lost his advantage. His reflexes were too slow, and he'd lost two

146

decisive seconds by stopping, paralyzed, and staring at it.

He shook his head to clear away the momentary shock. He gave up paying attention to the confused noise and blind milling of the crowd. He narrowed his concentration down to the girl and her gun. As far as he could permit himself to be concerned, he and she were alone in a private universe, each trying to overcome panic long enough to act.

He'd lost his aim, and his arm had dropped below the line of fire. He brought it up, deliberately slowing his impulse to fling it into position. If he missed, the odds would be all against a second shot.

It was a better aim than the conventional method, in any case. It permitted no elaboration; it had no grace or beauty, but it *was* a steadier method of aiming.

Her shot struck his forearm, and his hand slapped up into the air from the shock. His fingers almost lost their grip on the butt, and he clenched them convulsively.

The girl was tugging at her weapon, doing something with the buttplate.

His gun discharged into the air, and his arm shook with fresh pain from the recoil.

He could see the Accused was as wrought up as he was. He clutched his forearm with his left hand and steadied down. Before she could fire again, his gun burst into life, throwing her backward and down to the ground. She was obviously dead.

He took a deep, shuddering breath. The gun started to fall out of his weak fingers, but he caught it with his left hand and dropped it into its holster.

The world around him slowly filtered back into his senses. He became aware of angry shouts in the crowd of people, and of attendants struggling to hold them in check. There was a knot of people clustered around a family box, but before he could investigate that, he felt Kallimer put an arm around his waist and hold him up. He hadn't even realized he was swaying.

'We can't worry about the crowd,' Kallimer said in a peculiar voice. It was urgent, but he sounded calm under

147

it. There was no hysteria in him, and Joyce noted that to his credit.

'Did you see who threw the gun?' Joyce demanded.

Kallimer shook his head. 'No. Doesn't matter. We've got to get back to New York.'

Joyce looked up at the bench. Blanding wasn't in sight, but Pedersen was hanging by his hands, dangling down over its face, and dropping to the plaza. He bent, picked up the brief case he'd thrown down ahead of him, ripped it open, and pulled out his gun.

That was idiotic. What did he think he was doing?

'Joyce!' Kallimer was pulling at him.

'All right!' Joyce snapped in annoyance. He began to run toward Pedersen before the fool could disgrace himself. As he ran, he realized Kallimer was right. The three of them had to get back to New York as quickly as possible. The Bar Association had to know.

Pedersen sat far back in his corner of the train compartment, his eyes closed and his head against the paneling as though he was listening to the sound of the trolley running along the overhead cable. The Messire only knew what he was really listening to. His face was pale.

Joyce turned stiffly toward Kallimer, hampered by the sling and cast on his arm. The Associate was staring out the window, and neither he nor Pedersen had said a word since they'd boarded the train, fifteen minutes ago. At that time, there had still been noise coming from the plaza.

There'd been a twenty-minute wait for the train. That meant more than three-quarters of an hour had passed since the start of it all, and Joyce still did not understand exactly what had happened. He had only disconnected impressions of the entire incident, and, for the life of him, he could find no basic significance behind it, although he knew there had to be one.

'Kallimer.'

The Associate turned away from the window. 'What?'

Joyce gestured, conscious of his sudden inability to find the proper phrasing.

148

'You want to know what touched it off. Is that it?'

Joyce nodded, relieved at not having to say it after all.

Kallimer shook his head. 'I don't know, exactly. Somebody in the crowd felt strongly enough to throw her the gun. One of her relatives, I suppose.'

'But —' Joyce gestured inarticulately. 'It . . . it was a *legal* execution! Who would interfere with justice? Who'd take the risk of eternal damnation by interfering with The Messire's obvious will?'

Pedersen, in his corner, made a very peculiar sound. Kallimer shot him a cryptic glare. He turned back to Joyce and seemed to be searching for words.

'Joyce,' he said finally, 'how do you imagine The Messire would reverse a verdict of "Completely Guilty"?'

Joyce frowned. 'Well . . . I don't know. My gun might jam. Or I might fire and unaccountably miss.'

'You don't know for certain, because it's never happened. Am I correct?'

'Substantially.'

'Now. How many reversals have there been on verdicts of "Apparently Guilty"? When the Accused was given a gun with one cartridge in the chamber.'

'A few.'

'But it's never happened to any Justice you know, has it?'

Joyce shook his head. 'No, but there are recorded cases. A few, as I said.'

'Very well. What about 'Possibly Guilty'? Many reversals on those verdicts?'

'An appreciable number.'

'Almost had a few of those yourself, didn't you?'

'A few.'

'Very well.' Kallimer held up his hand, bending one finger for each point. 'Now – first we have the case in which the Accused is weaponless. No reversals. Next we have the case in which the Accused has one shot to fire. A few reversals. And finally we have the case in which the

149

Accused has as much of a weapon as the Presiding Justice. An appreciable number of reversals.

'Does it not seem to you, Justice Joyce, that this series of statistics might well occur without the intervention of any Divine Will whatsoever?'

Joyce stared at him, but Kallimer gave him no chance to reply.

'Furthermore, Joyce; do the people have the right to bear arms? That is to say, can you imagine an Accused who was acquainted with the firing and aiming of an automatic pistol? The answer – you asked, now hear me out – the answer is No.

'More. Have you ever heard of The Messire reversing a verdict of "Not Guilty"?'

Joyce bridled. 'There aren't two of those a year!'

Kallimer's mouth hooked. 'I know. But they *do* exist. Explain this, then; how do you reconcile Divine Will with the curious fact that verdicts of "Not Guilty" and "Completely Guilty" are *never* reversed, and never have been reversed, though Messire knows we came close this afternoon? Are you claiming that in those cases, every Justice who ever lived was right every time? Are you attempting to claim, for mortal men, the infallibility which is The Messire's particular province?'

Kallimer's face was tense with emotion, and Joyce received a distinct impression that the Associate was speaking with excessive violence; actually his voice was still under control.

'Mr Joyce, if you can't see the point I'm driving at, I am sorry. But, rest assured, somebody in that crowd of people finally realized it, after all these years. Somebody wasn't afraid of The Messire.' Kallimer turned his head sharply and looked out the window at the Hudson, running silver far below as the train swung over to the east shore. 'I'm not sure Pedersen wasn't right in drawing his gun. And, Mr Joyce, if what I've said hasn't shaken you, it certainly should have.'

Kallimer took a deep breath and seemed to calm down a little.

150

'Mr Joyce,' he said softly, 'I believe there's something you haven't thought of. I imagine it'll make you unhappy when I tell you.

'Talking in your terms, now – you don't have to give an inch, Mr Joyce; in fact, you have to hang on to your beliefs with absolute rigidity to appreciate the full impact – looking at it from your point of view: You can't imagine how The Messire would go about reversing an unjust verdict of 'Completely Guilty'. But The Messire is omniscient and omnipotent. His ways are complex and unknowable. Am I correct? Well, then, how do you know that what happened today wasn't a hint of how He'd manage it?'

The blood drained out of Joyce's face.

Late that night, Emily looked at him in surprise when she answered her door.

'Sam! But you never — ' She stopped. 'Come in, Sam. you surprised me.'

Joyce kissed her cheek and strode nervously into her apartment. He knew what had startled her. He never called on nights following trials; in the fifteen years they'd been together, she would naturally have noticed that. He considered the problem while on his way over, and the only thing to do, he'd decided, was to act as though nothing unusual were taking place. He reasoned that a woman, being a woman, would shrug her shoulders over it after the first few minutes. Probably, after a short time, she'd even begin to doubt her memory.

'Sam, what's the matter with your arm?'

He spun around and saw her still standing by the door, wearing a dressing gown, with her hair in curlers.

'Trial,' he bit off shortly. He paced across the room, took a pear out of a bowl, and bit into it. 'I'm hungry,' he said with false vigour.

She seemed to collect herself. 'Of course, Sam. I'll put something on the stove. It won't be more than a few moments. Excuse me.' She went into the kitchen, leaving him standing alone in the semidarkness surrounding the one light she'd switched on near the door. Impatiently, he snapped the switches of the other lamps in the room and stood in the middle of it, chewing the pear and bouncing it in his palm between bites.

He heard Emily put a pan on a burner. He moved abruptly and strode into the kitchen, stopping just inside the door and dropping the pear down the disposal chute.

'Finished it,' he said, explaining his presence. He looked around. 'Anything I can do?'

Emily looked up at him, a look of amused disbelief on her face, 'Sam, what's gotten into you?'

Joyce scowled. 'Anything wrong with coming up to see my girl?'

Saying it made the scowl disappear. He looked down at Emily, who was bent over the stove again. Fifteen years had touched her hair, and put little lines on her forehead and the corners of her mouth. They added a good bit to her lips and waist. But there was an earthly, commonsense comfort in her. He could put his key in the door at any time of night, and she'd hear the sound and be there to meet him.

He reached down and pulled her up. His arm twinged a bit, but that was unimportant at the moment. He folded his arms around her and cupped the back of her head in one palm. The warmth and security of her made his clutch tighter than he'd intended at the start. Suddenly he found himself wishing he'd never have to go back to his own ascetic flat.

Emily smiled faintly and kissed his chin. 'Sam, what *did* happen? I heard the trial results over the radio this afternoon, and all they announced for Nyack was a successful conclusion to a verdict of "Completely Guilty". Was there some trouble they didn't want to talk about?'

His mood burst, and he dropped his arms.

'What kind of trouble?' he asked sharply.

Her eyes opened, and she looked at him in fresh surprise. 'I didn't mean anything by it, Sam. Just ordinary trouble . . . you know, a lucky shot by the Accused — '

She looked at the light cast on his arm. 'But that couldn't be it, with an unarmed Accused — '

Joyce took an angry breath. 'I thought we had that clear between us,' he said in a voice he realized was too angry. 'From the very beginning, I've made it plain that your province is yours and my province is mine. If I don't tell you about it, you can assume I don't feel you should know.'

Emily stepped back and quickly bent over the stove again. 'All right, Sam,' she said in a low voice. 'I'm sorry.' She lifted the lid of a pan. 'Supper'll be ready in a minute. It'll be pretty busy in here when all these pots come to a boil at the same time.'

'I'll be waiting in the living room.' Joyce turned and walked out.

He paced back and forth over the rug, his lips in a tight line, conscious now of the pain in his arm.

One more scar. One more objection from The Messire. All safe in the end, but one more objection, nevertheless, and what did it mean?

And the Bar Association.

'A hearing!' he muttered. 'A full hearing tomorrow!' As though his report hadn't been adequate. He'd told them what happened. It should have been enough. But Kallimer, with his allegations that there was more to the incident —

Well, all right. Tomorrow he'd see about Kallimer.

Emily came into the living room. 'Supper's ready, Sam,' Her voice and expression were careful to be normal. She didn't want to provoke him again.

She was hurt, and he didn't like to see her that way. He laughed suddenly and put his arm around her shoulders, squeezing. 'Well, let's eat, eh, girl?'

'Of course, Sam.'

He frowned slightly, dissatisfied. But there was no point in trying to patch it up and only making it worse. He kept still as they went into the dining room.

They ate silently. Or rather, to be honest with himself, Joyce had to admit that he ate and Emily toyed with a small portion, keeping him company out of politeness.

The act of sitting still for twenty minutes quieted his

nerves a bit. And he appreciated Emily's courtesy. As he pushed his coffee cup away, he looked up at her and smiled.

'That was very good. Thank you, Emily.'

She smiled faintly. 'Thank you, Sam. I'm glad you liked it. I'm afraid it wasn't much. I hadn't planned — ' She broke off.

So, she *had* continued to wonder about his calling tonight. He smiled ruefully. And now she thought she'd offended him again. He'd been pretty grumpy tonight.

He reached out and took her hand. 'That's all right, Emily.'

After she'd washed the dishes, she came in and sat down beside him on the couch, where he was slumped with his feet on a hassock. His ankles and calves were aching. It was all right as long as he kept moving, but once he sat down the ache always began. He smiled at her wanly.

Smiling back, she bent wordlessly and began to massage his calves, working the muscles with her fingers.

'Emily — '

'Yes, Sam?'

'If . . . Nothing, Emily. There's not much point in talking about it.' He found himself caught between the desire to speak to someone and the urgent sense that this afternoon was best forgotten. He stared down past his feet without looking at anything. Perhaps there was some way to manoeuver her into telling him what he wanted to know, without his having to tell her about it.

Why was he reluctant to talk about this afternoon? He didn't know, exactly; but he couldn't bring himself to do it, no more than he could have discussed some character defect he might have accidentally observed in a lady or gentleman.

'What else did they say over the radio?' he asked without any special intonation. 'About Nyack.'

'Nothing, Sam, except for the bare results.'

He grunted in disappointment.

Perhaps there was some better angle of approach. 'Emily, suppose . . . suppose you knew of a case involving a people's girl and a family man. Suppose the girl had come up to the man on a public street and addressed him by his first name.'

He stopped uncomfortably.

'Yes, Sam?'

'Uh . . . well, what would you think?'

Emily's hands became still for a moment, then began working on his calves again.

'What would I think?' she asked in a low voice, looking down at the floor. 'I'd think she was very foolish.'

He grimaced. That wasn't what he wanted. But did he know what he wanted from her? What *was* the answer he was looking for? He tried again.

'Yes, of course. But, aside from that, what else?'

He saw Emily bite her lip. 'I'm afraid I don't understand what you mean, Sam.'

A tinge of his earlier anger put a bite in his voice. 'You're not that unintelligent, Emily.'

She took a deep breath and looked at him. 'Sam, something drastic went wrong today, didn't it? Something very bad. You were terribly upset when you came in — '

'Upset? I don't think so,' he interrupted quickly.

'Sam, I've been your mistress for fifteen years.'

He knew his face was betraying him. In her flashes of shrewdness, she always did this to him. She'd put her finger exactly on the vulnerable truth, disarming his ability to cover up.

He sighed and spread his hands in a gesture of resignation. 'All right, Emily. Yes, I am upset.' The irritation welled up again. 'That's why I want some help from you, instead of this evasiveness.'

She straightened up, taking her hands off his aching legs, and half-turned on the couch, so that she was looking directly into his eyes. She held his gaze without hesitation.

'Maybe you're asking too much of me. Perhaps not. This *is* important, isn't it? I've never seen you quite as troubled as this.'

She was tense, he realized. Tense, and apprehensive. But

he saw, as well, that she had decided to go ahead, despite whatever her private doubts might be.

'Yes,' he admitted, 'it's important.'

'Very well. You want to know what I think about that girl? Suppose you tell me what you think, first. Do you believe she did it out of spite, or malice, or impulse?'

He shook his head. 'Of course not! She was in love with him, and forgot herself.'

Emily's eyes welled up with a sudden trace of tears. Joyce stared at her, dumbfounded, for the few seconds before she wiped one hand across her eyes in annoyance.

'Well?' she asked in a low voice.

'I'm afraid it's my turn not to understand,' he said after a moment. He frowned. What was she driving at?

'What distinguishes me from that girl, Sam? A few years? What do you expect me to think?'

'It's not the same thing at all, Emily!' he shot back in honest anger. 'Why . . . why you're a mature woman. We're — '

He couldn't really point out the difference, but he knew it was there. She'd never said or done anything —

'Emily, you know very well you'd never do what that girl did!'

'Only because I'm more conscious of the rules,' she answered in a low voice. 'What real difference is there between her and myself? It is that it's you and I, rather than two other people; rather than any one of the scores of similar couples we know? What distinguishes us in your eyes? The fact that we're not a case for you to try?'

'Emily, this is ridiculous!'

She shook her head slowly. 'That girl broke the law. I haven't. But I haven't only because I realized, from the very start, just what kind of tight-rope I'd be walking for the rest of our lives. I couldn't leave you and go back to the people, now; I've grown too used to living as I do. But I'll always be no more than I was born to.

'Suppose I were a People's man – a mechanic, or perhaps even an engineer if I'd bound myself to some family. I'd know that all my skill and training wouldn't be of any use if I were accused of some crime in a court of law. I'd know that addressing my patron in public by his first name would be a crime – a different kind of crime than if I were my patron's mistress, certainly, but a crime, nevertheless. Let's assume that, as my patron's engineer, I overrode his will on the specifications for whatever product my patron manufactured. Or that I attempted to redesign a product or develop a new one without first getting his approval and suggestions; that would be legally analogous to what the girl did, wouldn't it?'

'Yes, and properly so,' Joyce retorted.

Emily looked at him and nodded slowly. She went on:

'If I were that engineer, and I had any common sense, I'd be constantly aware of the difference between myself and my patron. I would remind myself, every day, that my patron was born to a family, and that my patron would, in turn, be permitted the sacrament of marriage when he desired it with a lady. I would understand that engineers were members of the people, and that my patron was a member of one of the First Families, or a Legislator, or a Justice. Realizing all this, I would always be careful never to encroach on the difference between us, accepting my fate in having been born to the people, and his having been born to a family.'

Joyce frowned. 'That sounds a little bit as though you considered birth a blind accident.'

'Emily looked at him silently. She took a deep breath. 'Being an intelligent person, I, as that engineer, would attribute my station at birth to the direction of The Messire. You'll hear no heresies from me, Sam.' She reached out and took his hand.

'That's why I'll say, again, that the girl in Nyack was foolish. That *was* the case in Nyack, wasn't it? She did what none of us, in our right minds, would consider doing. Certainly, she did what I'd never do, but then, I'm older than she. I was older when I came to you, or I at least assume so, since you called her a girl.'

Suddenly, she bit her lip. 'Young people in love are not necessarily in their right minds, just as people enraged are not acting logically. Who's to say what their punishment should be?'

'There is Someone,' Joyce answered firmly.

Emily nodded, looking at him, her expression abstracted. Suddenly she said:

'Sam, have you ever really looked at yourself in a mirror? Not to see whether you'd shaved properly, or whether your wig was crooked on the morning before a trial, but just to look at yourself.'

He couldn't understand this new tack.

'Do you know you have a very young face, Sam? Under that black beard-shadow, with the scowl gone, you've got the face of a troubled adolescent. You've taught yourself dignity, and put flesh on your body, but you're still a young boy, searching for the key that will wind the world up to run accurately forever. Perhaps you believe you've found it. You believe in what you're doing. You believe that justice is the most important thing in the world. What you do, you do as a crusade. There's no wanton malice or cruelty in you. I don't believe I've ever known you to do anything purely for yourself.

'I love you for it, Sam. But, except sometimes with me, you've submerged yourself in your ideal, until you've learned to ignore Sam Joyce entirely. You're Mister Justice Joyce all the time.'

She closed her hand on his. 'Something happened this afternoon, and I suspect it was drastic. You've come to me after facing an unarmed Accused – a girl, young and unskilled – but there's a cast on your arm, and what must be a bullet hole under it. I don't know what happened. I do know there's a news blackout on Nyack.

'Sam, if the system's been finally challenged, then you're in terrible danger. Other men aren't like you. Other men – people's men and family men – act in rage, or fear, or love. If they tear down your world and your ideal —'

'Tear down — !'

'. . . If they tear down what you have given your life to, there will be nothing left of you. If the system goes, it takes

158

Justice Joyce's lifeblood with it, and only I know where the little fragment of Sam Joyce lives. It won't be enough.'

'Emily, you're exaggerating beyond all reason!'

Emily clutched his hand. He saw, to his complete amazement, that she'd shut her eyes against the tears, but that streaks of silent moisture were trickling down her cheeks.

'You've come to me for help, but I'm part of the world, too, and I have to live the way it lets me. After all these years, you want to know whether you've been right, and I'm supposed to tell you.

'I told you I thought the girl was foolish. Sam, I love you, but I don't dare give you your answer. I told you: you won't hear any heretical statements from me.'

The night had slowly edged into dawn. Joyce stared at it through the window beside the bed. He had no way of knowing whether Emily had ever gone to sleep or not. She was lying motionless, just as she had been all night.

Joyce's eyes were burning, and the short stubble of his graying natural hair was thick with perspiration. The night had been sleepless for him.

His arm was much better this morning, but he still remembered the shock of the bullet.

If you believed, as you must believe, that The Messire saw every human deed, knew every human thought, and caused every human event, then what had He meant in Nyack?

If the sentence was correct, why did The Messire permit her that one shot? Why hadn't whoever threw the gun been stopped before he could do it? If the sentence was unjust, why hadn't she killed him?

Was it that The Messire approved of him, but not of the basis of his judgment? But his basis was the Law, and The Messire had handed down the Law!

Was it, as Kallimer had said, that The Messire was not as Joyce conceived of him?

What did Emily think?

He reminded himself that what Emily thought was irrelevant, as he had hastily reminded himself many times during the past night. Her opinion did not govern the truth or falsehood of justice. Justice was an absolute; it was either right, no matter what the opinions of Mankind, or it was worthless.

Was it, as Kallimer had said viciously, that The Messire was trying to make him understand something?

What?

What had He meant in Nyack?

Joyce lay on the bed, exhausted. He knew he was thinking wildly. He'd gone over and over this ground, trying to find the proper logic, and accomplishing nothing. He was in no condition to reason correctly. He only hoped he could act wisely at the hearing this afternoon.

He slipped cautiously out of bed, hesitating at every rustle of the sheets. Once out, he dressed hastily, and left the apartment as quietly as he could. He didn't want Emily to wake up and see what condition he was in.

He walked into the hearing room with measured steps, hoping no one would notice his unsettled state of mind. When the Chief Justice showed agitation, what could anyone expect of the lesser Justices?

This, too, was part of the task, and the young, ambitious Associate Justice of Utica hadn't had the faintest inkling of it, just as, throughout his dedicated advancement through the ranks of his profession, he could not have dreamed how difficult it would some day be to walk steadily through a door when sleepless legs and aching ankles dragged at every step.

He saw the tension rampant in every Member. No one was sitting down quietly, waiting for the hearing to begin. Knots of men stood everywhere, talking sharply, and there was a continual movement from one group to another.

Joyce scowled in annoyance and nodded shortly as most of the faces in the room were turned toward him. He looked around for Joshua Normandy, but the Bar Association's Chairman had not yet come in. He saw Kallimer, standing to one side, wearing his frown and talking alone to a white-faced Pedersen.

Joyce went over to them. He hadn't decided yet what to do with Kallimer. The man was arrogant. He seemed to derive genuine pleasure from talking in terms Joyce was unable to understand. But the man was intelligent, and ambitious. His ambition would lead him to defend the same principles that Joyce defended, and his intelligence would make him a superlative Chief Justice, once Joyce was gone.

For the sake of that, Joyce was willing to let yesterday's questionable behavior go. Perhaps, after all, Kallimer had been right in asking for a reconsideration of the verdict.

Once again, Joyce was painfully conscious of his inability to arrive at any firm opinion on yesterday's events. He stopped in front of Kallimer and Pedersen with a shake of his head, and only then realized how peculiar the gesture must look to them.

'Good afternoon, Justice,' Kallimer said dryly.

Joyce searched his face for some indication of his state of mind, but there was nothing beyond the omnipresent frown.

'Good afternoon, Justices,' he said finally. 'Or have the election results been confirmed, Legislator?' he asked Pedersen.

Pedersen's face was strained. 'Yes, sir. The results were confirmed. But I resigned.'

Joyce's eyebrows shot up. Recovering, he tried to smile pleasantly. 'Then you're returning to the Bar?'

Pedersen shook his head. 'No . . . uh —' he husked in a dry voice, 'I'm here simply as a witness to . . . uh . . . yesterday.' He was deathly pale.

Kallimer smiled coldly. 'Mr Pedersen has decided to retire from public life, Justice Joyce. He now considers that his first attempt to dissociate himself from the Bar was inadequate.'

Joyce looked from Kallimer back to Pedersen. The younger man, he suddenly realized, was terrified.

'Blanding's dead, you know,' Kallimer said without inflection. 'A paving block was thrown at his head yesterday afternoon. It's uncertain just what the circumstances were but a member of the Civil Guard brought the word out.' Kallimer smiled at Pedersen. 'And now our former Associate, his earlier presentiments proven correct, is shortly taking a trip abroad – the Lakes Confederation, I believe?'

'I have distant relations in St Paul,' Pedersen confirmed huskily. 'And there is an Ontario branch of the family in Toronto. I plan to be away for some time. A tour.'

Kallimer still smiled. 'The key word in that statement would be "distant", would it not, Mr Pedersen?'

Pedersen flushed angrily, but Joyce seized on Kallimer's attitude as a reassuring sign. At least, Pedersen's cowardice wasn't general. For the moment, that seemed more important than the news of Blanding's death.

His lack of astonishment made him look at himself in wonder. Was he that much upset, that a Justice's murder failed to shock him? Was he really that far gone in his acceptance of the incredible?

He knew, with a calmly logical part of his mind, that before yesterday he would have considered himself insane to even think of anyone's attacking the Law. Today, he could pass over it. Not lightly, but, nevertheless, pass over it.

'You're sure of your information, Kallimer?' he asked.

Kalimer nodded, looking at him curiously. 'The witness is reliable. And he brought out the gun, too. That's an astonishing item in itself. You'll be interested.'

Joyce raised his eyebrows politely. 'Really?' He saw Joshua Normandy come into the hearing room, and nodded in the Chairman's direction. 'The hearing's about to begin. It'll be brought up, of course?'

Kallimer was frankly puzzled by his attitude. Joyce's head was erect, and his shoulders had abruptly straightened out of their unconscious slump.

'Yes, of course.'

'Good. Shall we take our places? Good afternoon, Mr Pedersen. It was a pleasure, having you on my bench.' He took Kallimer's arm, and, together, they strolled up to the long table facing the chairs of the lesser Justices.

Joyce knew what was happening to him, and the calm, judicial part of his mind, at last given something it understood to work with, approved.

162

He had been in a panic. At noon, yesterday, the foundations of his logic had been destroyed. The integrity of justice and Justices had been attacked, and his belief in the universal acceptance of The Messire's Law had been proved false. He had discovered, in one climactic instant, that there were people willing to deliberately attack the Law.

He had been beyond his depth. He had no precedent for such a crime; no basis on which to judge the situation. Someone else, perhaps, such as Kallimer or Justice Normandy, might have the reach of mind to encompass it. But Joyce knew he was not a brilliant man. He was only an honest man, and he knew what was beyond him. In the instant that he had stopped, staring dumbfounded at the gun lying on the plaza stones, with the Accused reaching for it eagerly, he had stopped being capable of evaluating the legal situation and taking steps to rectify it. Panic could warp a man's judgment completely.

That was what The Messire had been trying to make him realize. The world was changing, and the Chief Justice was not equipped to deal with the change.

As an honest man; as a man sincere in his beliefs, he was ready to give up his responsibilities and let the better suited men take them up.

He nodded to Justice Normandy and the other Bar Association officers. Then he sat down calmly, with Kallimer beside him, and waited to see what the more intelligent men had made of the situation.

Kallimer was holding up the gun brought out of Nyack. Joyce looked at it curiously.

It was late in the afternoon, and a good deal of testimony had already been recorded. Pedersen stated that he was aware of angry movement in the crowd as Joyce made his draw, but that the gun had been thrown by an unidentified man before anything could be done. After the shooting, the man and a surrounding group of other men had been lost in the crowd. The crowd itself had been bewildered at first, and then divided in its reactions. That early in the riot, there had been no signs of unanimous effort.

The Civil Guardsman had testified that, as far as he

knew, he was the only survivor of the squad detailed to keep order during the trial. He had seized the gun after the executed Accused dropped it, and run to Guard headquarters for help. It was his impression that the immediate deaths among family members at the trial were the result of spontaneous riot in the crowd, and not of any organized plan of assassination.

Justice Kallimer had commented that this was also his impression. The only traces of intelligent planning, he stated, had shown themselves in the cutting of the train cables out of Nyack and the attack on the radio station, where the supervising family man had smashed the transmitter before it could be captured. Note was made of the loyalty of the station engineering staff.

Now, Kallimer said: 'Bearing previous testimony in mind, I'd like to call this hearing's attention to the construction and design of this illegal weapon.'

Joyce bent closer. There were a number of peculiarities in the gun, and they interested him.

'First,' Kallimer went on, 'the weapon is obviously handmade. Its frame consists of a solid metal piece – steel, I'm told by a competent engineer – which bears obvious file marks. Moreover, it is of almost primitive design. It has a smoothbore barrel, drilled through from muzzle to breech, and is mortised at the breech to accommodate one hand-inserted cartridge and a spring-loaded hammer. Additional cartridges are stored in the butt, covered by a friction plate. It is fired by thumbing back the hammer and releasing it, after which the fired cartridge case must be removed by hand before it can be reloaded.

'A hasty weapon. A weapon of desperation, thrown together by someone with only a few hours to work in.'

Kallimer put the gun down. 'A hopelessly inefficient and inadequate weapon. I am informed that the barrel was not even drilled parallel to the frame's long axis, and that the crude sights were also askew, further complicating the error in aiming. It is remarkable that Mr Justice Joyce was struck at all, and it is no wonder at all that the Accused was never able to fire a second shot.'

Joyce shook his head slightly. It was perfectly obvious how the girl had managed to hit him. But then, Kallimer, with his slightly eccentric viewpoint, would not be likely to take The Messire into account.

Kallimer was speaking again.

'The point, however, isn't relevant here. It is the nature of this weapon which concerns us. Obviously, it was not constructed by anyone particularly skilled in the craft, and its design is hopelessly unimaginative. It is unlikely that any others exist. It follows, then, that the rebellion, if I may call it such for the moment, is largely confined to the Accused's immediate . . . ah . . . relations. No actual large-scale, organized effort exists.

'We have the testimony of Mr Pedersen and the Guardsman. It seems obvious that the gun-throwers' plans culminated in the delivery of the weapon to the Accused. What followed was a spontaneous demonstration. This, together with some other relevant data already mentioned in testimony, is the basis on which we have formulated our program of rectification.'

Kallimer turned toward the center of the table. 'Justice Normandy.'

Normandy was an aged, gray-headed man whose heavy brows hung low over his eyes. He rose out of his chair and supported his weight on his hands, leaning out over the table and looking toward the lesser Justices in their seats.

Joyce looked at him curiously.

Normandy had never been Chief Justice. He'd risen to Chief Associate under Kemple, the Chief Justice before the one Joyce had replaced. The oldest son of one of the First Families, Normandy had then retired from active work, becoming first Recorder and then Chairman of the Bar Association. He'd held the position longer than Joyce had been Chief Justice, and he was at least seventy.

Joyce wondered what he and Kallimer had decided to do.

Normandy's voice was harsh with age. He forced each word out of his throat.

'Justice Kallimer has summed up very well. A purely personal rebellion against the Law in Nyack has touched off a spontaneous demonstration. You've noticed the lack of evidence implicating any ringleaders except the Accused's relations. They're nothing but woodworkers. There was some later participation by engineers, because it took training to see the importance of cutting off communications. But that wasn't until this emotional upheaval had a chance to get contagious.

'There's a certain rebellious feeling, yes. But it's hardly born yet. It won't spread unless we let it, and we won't. By tomorrow afternoon, we'll be back to normal.

'Thank you, Justices. This hearing's concluded, and Mr Joyce, Mr Kallimer, and I will stay behind for further discussion.'

Joyce watched the lesser Justices file out of the hearing room, their manner much less nervous than it had been. Normandy had put some starch back into their spines.

Joyce, too, felt better. He'd been right in expecting Kallimer and Normandy to have a solution. He was leaving the Law in capable hands.

Normandy waited until the room was empty. Then he turned to Kallimer with an expression of disgust.

'Well, they believed it. I'd be happier if a few of them hadn't.'

Kallimer shrugged. 'There's no telling. If any of them saw through it, they'd be intelligent enough not to show it.'

Normandy cocked an eyebrow, pursed his lips, and, after a moment, grinned. 'That's a good point.'

Joyce looked blankly at both of them. 'I gather,' he said finally, 'that the situation is more serious than was divulged.' He felt a slight return of his old disquiet, but nothing near panic.

Normandy and Kallimer turned in their chairs. Both of them looked at him speculatively.

Normandy nodded. 'By quite a good bit. It took the

engineers a while to realize what was happening, but they took over the rebellion within the first hour. They're directing it now. We had to bomb the radio-station and establish a false transmitter on the same wave length. It looks very much as though the engineers had a plan ready to use, but not quite this soon. They were caught a little short.'

Normandy grimaced. 'Not short enough, though. We anticipated a little trouble down there, but we were unprepared for the discovery of anything like that. The Guard can't handle it. I sent in the Army this morning.'

Kallimer grunted. 'You know,' he told Normandy, 'I asked Joyce to reconsider his verdict.'

Normandy's eyes snapped open. 'You did? Why?'

'We didn't need any tests, after all. I could smell the trouble in that crowd. It was that thick. They didn't know it themselves, but they were spoiling for a riot.' He shrugged. 'Joyce overruled me, of course. It's a good thing, too, or we'd never have found out in time just how deep the trouble had dug.'

Normandy stared thoughtfully off into distance, his head barely moving as he nodded to himself. 'Yes,' he whispered under his breath.

He looked sharply at Joyce. 'How much of this shocks you, Justice?'

Joyce was looking at the expression on Kallimer's face. It had become coldly sardonic.

'I — ' He broke off and shrugged in reply to Normandy's question. 'I don't really know. But I'm sure you're aware of what you're doing.' Nevertheless, he was bewildered. He couldn't quite make out what Kallimer had meant.

Normandy looked at him steadily, his black eyes watchful. 'I've always been of two minds about you,' he said in a thoughtful voice. 'I believe I chose wisely, but there's no certainty, with individuals like you.' He grinned in his abrupt way. 'But sometimes a calculated risk is justified. Sometimes, only an honest man will do.'

Joyce's bewilderment was growing. He understood that Normandy was being much more candid with him than he had ever been before. Vaguely, he was aware that the situation had forced Normandy into it.

But if *Normandy* was being forced into drastic steps, then what did that say about Sam Joyce's ability to do the proper thing in this crisis?

'There's something I believe I should tell you,' he said quickly, conscious of a return to his earlier panic. He had to state his position as early in this discussion as possible, before Normandy and Kallimer assumed he could be counted on. 'I'm . . . not sure of exactly what you mean about me,' he went on as Normandy and Kallimer looked at him curiously. 'But there's something you should know.'

He stopped to choose his words carefully. He had to convince these men that he wasn't acting on impulse; that he'd thought this out. They deserved an explanation, after having assumed he'd help them. And, too, it was important to him personally. Possibly this was the most important decision of his life.

'I've been Chief Justice for a comparatively long time,' he began. He had; he'd always felt The Messire had a good servant in him, and, up until yesterday, The Messire had seemed to agree.

He looked down at his hands. 'I have a good record. I've done my best.

'You know my history. I began years ago, on a minor bench, and I rose step by step. No one has the skill with his gun or is better in the ritual of Trial than I was in my prime.' He looked up at Normandy and Kallimer, trying to see whether they understood him. 'I feel that I've been a good Justice; that I've served The Messire's Law as He desired it. But I've always known I wasn't the most brilliant man on the bench. I haven't delivered many famous opinions, and I'm no lawyer's lawyer. I've simply' – he gestured indecisively – 'been a Justice for a long time.' He paused momentarily.

'But this,' he went on in a low voice, 'is beyond my capabilities.' He looked down again. 'I know I haven't the capacity to do my duty properly in this situation. I'd like to resign in Justice Kallimer's favor.'

There was a long silence. Joyce did not look up, but sat thinking of the foolish things he'd done and thought during the past two days.

He looked up, finally, and saw Normandy's quizzled expression. Kallimer's face was a nonplussed blank.

Normandy tented his fingers and blew out a breath over them. 'I see.' He looked cryptically at Kallimer, and Kallimer seemed to exchange some silent message with him.

Kallimer spoke slowly. 'Mr Joyce, I know you well enough to realize this hasn't been a hasty decision. Would you mind telling me what led you to it?'

Joyce shook his head. 'Not at all. I've decided that this is the only possible interpretation of yesterday's events in the plaza. It seems clear to me that The Messire's intent was to have me do what I've just done.'

Normandy jerked his head violently, and stared at Joyce. 'I'll be damned!' he exploded.

Kallimer's mouth twisted. 'This is hardly what I expected to result from our talk yesterday,' he muttered. He looked at Joyce with perverse admiration. Then he spoke to Normandy. 'Well, Justice, there's your honest man.'

Normandy shot Kallimer one sour look before he turned back to Joyce. His voice grated harshly.

'That's all well and good, but you're not resigning. Not now, at least, and never in Kallimer's favor. You've still got one Trial to run, and Kallimer's after my job, not yours.'

'Not until after you've retired, Justice,' Kallimer interjected, turning his sardonic smile on Normandy. 'I've made it clear I have no intention of competing with *you*. Furthermore, I'm your only natural heir in any case.' He chuckled for the first time in Joyce's experience. 'There aren't many like us born to each generation, are there, Justice?'

Joyce sat numbly, unable to decide what he thought of Normandy's outburst.

'Justice Normandy — ' he said finally.

'What?'

'You say I've still got one Trial— '

'Yes!'

'But, if The Messire has indicated that He no longer considers me competent, the Trial will be prejudiced — '

Normandy thrust himself out of his chair and away from the table. His eyes were blazing, and his hands trembled. 'Damn your Messire! He didn't meddle with your last trial, did he?'

'Sir?'

Normandy cursed again and turned away. 'Kallimer, talk to this moron! I've had enough.' He stalked out of the hearing room, and the door crashed behind him.

Kallimer was looking after him with a faint look of exasperation tingeing the amusement of his mouth.

'He's getting old, Joyce.' Kallimer sighed. 'Well, I suppose the day will come when I'll have no more patience, either. It's a shaky pedestal he sits on.'

Joyce was in a turmoil. He knew his face was pale.

Kallimer turned back to him. 'There's been an insertion made in your court calendar,' he told him. 'Tomorrow, you'll hold a special mass trial for the engineers the Army will be dragging out of Nyack. They'll be indicted as "members of the people". Their origin won't be specified – no use alarming the nation. Is there? And I suppose there'll be a variety of charges. I'll set them up tonight. But the vedict'll be "Completely Guilty" in every case. You and I and a couple of other Justices will handle the executions.'

Joyce found himself unable to argue with more than the last few statements. Too much was happening.

'A mass trial? Here, in New York, you mean. For the Nyack rebels. But that's illegal!'

Kallimer nodded. 'So are improper indictment and prejudged verdict. But so is rebellion.

'This folderol of Normandy's has a rather shrewd point. The rebels will be punished, but the general populace won't know what for. Only the other rebellious organizations scattered throughout the country will realize what's happened. It'll slow down their enthusiasm, giving us time to root them out.'

Joyce looked down at the floor to hide the expression on

his face. Kallimer seemed not at all concerned with breaking the spirit of the Law. Normandy was even more blunt than that.

It was a frightening step in his logic, but there was only one possible answer. Both of them were acting as though man made the Law, and men administered the final verdict; as though there were no Messire.

He looked up at Kallimer, wondering what his face was showing of the sudden emptiness in his stomach. He felt as though he was looking down at the Associate from a great height, or up from the bottom of a pit.

'What did Normandy mean about my last trial?' he asked in a low voice.

'First of all, Joyce, bear in mind that The Messire is omniscient. He knows of more crimes than we possibly can. Even if we judge a case incorrectly, it is possible our verdict is nevertheless justified by some other crime of the Accused's.'

He looked at Joyce with a flicker of anxiety flashing subtly across his face, leaning even closer, and Joyce's first emptiness became a twinge of disgust and sickness.

'I accept that,' Joyce said, the words tasting cottony in his mouth, but wanting to urge Kallimer on.

Kallimer twitched his shoulders. 'Perhaps you do,' he muttered. Joyce appreciated, with a deep, bitter amusement that never came to the surface, just how much Kallimer must hate Normandy for leaving him with this task to perform.

'In any case,' Kallimer went on, 'about the girl, yesterday; Normandy's son had heard some things from her. A lot of unrest in Nyack; talk; dissatisfaction; that sort of thing. He told his father.

'It wasn't the only place we'd heard that from, but it was our real lead. It was decided that a trial, with a particularly controversial member of the people as the Accused, might bring enough of it to the surface for us to gauge its importance.'

He stopped and shook his head. 'It certainly did. We

171

hadn't the faintest idea it was that strong, or that close to exploding. Sheer luck we found it out.'

Joyce looked steadily at Kallimer, hoping his face was calm. 'The girl wasn't guilty.'

Kallimer's mouth twitched. 'Not of the charge we tried her on, no. Normandy's son accused her on his father's orders. You were sent down to try the case because we could predict you'd give us the verdict we wanted. I went along to observe.'

Joyce nodded slowly. 'I think I understand now,' he said.

In the middle of the day, just at noon, Samson Joyce stood at the foot of the high steps behind New York City's onyx judges' bench.

'Ready, Justice?' Kallimer asked him.

'Yes,' Joyce answered. He replaced the ceremonial gun in its tooled holster.

Kallimer looked at him again and shook his head. 'Justice, if we weren't in public, I'd offer you my hand. You hit bottom and you've come up swinging.'

Joyce's lower lip tugged upward at the corners. 'Thank you, Justice,' he said, and prepared to walk up the steps on his aching legs.

Emily had been puzzled, too, as he prepared to leave her this morning.

'Sam, I can't understand you,' she'd said worriedly, watching him scowl with pain as he stood up from putting on his boots.

He smiled at her, ignoring the ache in his legs. 'Why?'

'You haven't slept in two nights, now. I know something new happened yesterday.'

He bent and kissed her, still smiling.

'Sam, what is it?' she asked, the tears beginning to show at the corners of her eyes. 'You're too calm. And you won't talk to me.'

He shrugged. 'Perhaps I'll tell you about it later.'

The steps seemed almost inhumanly high today, though

he'd walked up them often. He reached the center of the bench gratefully, and leaned against the parapet. Looking down, he saw the Accused standing in their box. They'd been given new clothing, and an attempt had been made to hide their bandages. They were a sullen, dun-colored knot of men and women.

He looked across the plaza at the First Family boxes, crowded with the family men and their ladies, and the lesser family boxes flanking them. There was the usual overflow crowd of people, too, and a doubled force of Civil Guards.

The Accused, the First Families, the lesser families, the people, and even some of the Civil Guards, were all watching him. For all that a number of Justices would go through the full ritual of Trial today, he was the only one who wore the Suit.

When he'd come home to Emily last night, she'd asked him what had happened, looking up at his calm face.

'I went to Chapel after the hearing,' he'd told her, and now he seemed to stand there again.

'Lowery, one of Manhattan's Associate Justices, began to read the indictments. It was only then that Joyce realized there'd been applause for him and his Associates, and that he'd automatically instructed Lowery to begin.

He listened to the solemn beat of the words in the plaza.

This was Trial. Once again, men stood before The Messire, and, once again, the Justices endeavored to act as proper instruments of His justice.

Thirty years of trials had brought him here, in his Suit. In that time, The Messire had thought well of him.

But Kallimer and Normandy had planted the dirty seed of doubt in his mind, and though he knew them for what they were, still, the doubt was there. If the girl had been innocent, how had he been permitted to execute his unjust sentence upon her?

Kallimer had given him an answer for that, but Kallimer had given him too many answers already. It wasn't until he stood in Chapel, watching the candles flicker, that he understood where the test would lie.

If there was no Messire – the thought bewildered him, but he clung to it for argument's sake – then every particle of his life was false, and the ideal he served was dust.

If there was an Ultimate Judge – and how many noons, in thirty years, had brought him the feeling of communion with his Judge – then Joyce knew where to make his appeal.

He looked across the plaza at Joshua Normandy's box, and reflected that Normandy could not begin to guess the magnitude of what was undergoing Trial today.

He put his hand inside his vest and closed his fingers around the butt of his Grennell. It was his gun. It had served him as he had served The Messire; efficiently, without question.

Here was where the test came; here where men prayed to The Messire for the ultimate, infallible judgment.

The Messire knew the guilty, and the innocent; punished the one and protected the other. Joyce was only His instrument, and Trial the opportunity for His judgment to become apparent.

He whispered to himself: 'I pray my verdict is correct, but if it is not, I pray that justice prevail at this trial.' He took out the gun.

He turned quickly, and fired in Kallimer's direction. He fired across the plaza at Joshua Normandy. Then he began to fire at random into the First Family boxes, seeing Normandy collapse in his box, hearing Kallimer's body tumble backward off the bench, and knowing, whether he was right or wrong, that whatever happened now, The Messire had not, at least, reversed his verdict.

This was the Truth he'd lived for.

Threads of Time

Edited by Robert Silverberg

Three stunning novellas, written specially for this collection, each exploring a different facet of time . . .

Gregory Benford's *Threads of Time* unearths, in the wreckage of a crashed alien ship, a memory bank that goes back millions of years and contains some pretty startling revelations.

Clifford D. Simak's *The Marathon Photograph* is the story of a quiet man's journey into time and the extraordinary evidence he brought back with him to prove where he'd been.

And Norman Spinrad's fabled classic *Riding the Torch*, where the only relief from the endless tedium of space flight is to go out alone into the black void of infinite time and infinite space.

The Time Hoppers

Robert Silverberg

They'd been turning up in other centuries for a long time now: men from the 25th century whose only escape from the pressures of a totally controlled environment was to travel backwards in time to another era. They'd raised children, performed great deeds. In short, they'd become a part of history. But now it was 2490 and the date they'd time-hopped from was fast approaching.

Was their disappearance back into time inevitable? What if they were prevented from vanishing when the time came? Would history simply collapse? Would centuries of human achievement be wiped off the records?

Robert Silverberg – one of the true geniuses of science fiction – juggles with the devastating paradoxes of time travel in a classic, gripping novel of suspense and adventure.